Chestnut Ridge Acres

Books by Carrie Bender

Miriam's Journal Series

A Fruitful Vine
A Winding Path
A Joyous Heart
A Treasured Friendship
A Golden Sunbeam
Miriam's Cookbook

WHISPERING BROOK SERIES

Whispering Brook Farm
Summerville Days
Chestnut Ridge Acres
Hemlock Hill Hideaway

Dora's Diary Series

Birch Hollow Schoolmarm
Lilac Blossom Time

Chestnut
Ridge Acres

Carrie Bender

Herald
Press

Scottdale, Pennsylvania
Waterloo, Ontario

Library of Congress Cataloging-in-Publication Data
Bender, Carrie, date.
    Chestnut Ridge Acres / Carrie Bender.
        p. cm.—(Whispering Brook series ; 3)
    Summary: Joe and Arie, a young Amish couple, try to get
through their first summer on their farm with the help of
Joe's younger sister Nancy and brother Steven.
        ISBN 0-8361-9077-7 (alk. paper)
        [1. Amish—Fiction. 2. Farm life—Fiction. 3. Family—life—
Fiction.] I. Title. II. Series: Bender, Carrie, date.
Whispering Brook series ; 3.
PZ7.B43136Ch   1997   97-22082
[Fic]—dc21

CHESTNUT RIDGE ACRES
Copyright © 1997 by Herald Press, Scottdale, Pa. 15683
      Published simultaneously in Canada by Herald Press,
      Waterloo, Ont. N2L 6H7. All rights reserved
Library of Congress Catalog Number: 97-22082
International Standard Book Number: 0-8361-9077-7
Printed in the United States of America
Cover art and illustrations by Joy Dunn Keenan
Book design by Paula Johnson

06 05 04 03 02 01 00 10 9 8 7 6 5 4 3 2
12,400 copies in print

To order or request information, please call
1-800-759-4447 (individuals); 1-800-245-7894 (trade).
Website: www.mph.org

*To
my
family*

Note

This story is fiction,
but true to Amish life.
Any resemblance to persons
living or dead is coincidental.

Contents

1

The Big Day

NANCY Petersheim stretched and yawned lazily under the woolen comforter she shared with her younger sister Susie. She snuggled cozily under its warmth and burrowed deeper into the folds. It was too early to get up, the room was still dark, and Jeremiah the rooster wasn't crowing yet.

Usually she slept until she heard the familiar chug-chug when *Daed* (Dad) started the diesel power unit for milking, and then she would think about getting up. Until *Mamm* (Mom) called her, she would revel in the soft luxury of her comfortable bed.

Down the hall, the boys' door opened, and hurried footsteps passed the girls' room. "Wake up, you *Schlofkopps* (sleepyheads)," Steven called. "Today's the big day!"

Nancy sprang out of bed. How could she have forgotten? Today was Tuesday, Joe and Arie's wedding day! Shivering in the chilly November morning coolness, she went to the window and peered out. Yes, the stars were shining. No snow today.

"Wake up, Susie," she sang out. "We don't want to be late today. You can help me feed the chickens and the calves."

Sleepily, Susie crawled out of bed, and Nancy helped her unbutton her long flannel nightgown. Then she dressed quickly while Susie scampered downstairs to dress in front of the big black kitchen range. Little Lydia was already up, too, and dressing in front of the stove.

Mamm was riddling the ashes down and opening the draft on the stove. The glowing coals would soon have the kitchen toasty warm. "Where's Joe?" Nancy asked as she came into the kitchen, pinning on her apron. "He didn't leave already, did he?"

"He's just hitching up Chief now," Mamm replied. "He wants to make sure he'll be the first one at the Millers. He'll leave as soon as he's eaten breakfast."

Nancy grabbed her coat and scarf from the row of hooks behind the stove and dashed out the door. Joe was backing Chief into the buggy shafts, and Nancy sprang to fasten the traces and backing strap on one side. "It might be the last chance I have to help you hitch up," she joked. "After this, you'll always have Arie to help."

Joe smiled as he tied Chief to the railing and blanketed him. "Not if you come and work for us like you

10

did for Mary and Jacob," he replied. "You like to milk cows, don't you?"

"I'm afraid I won't get the chance," Nancy said wistfully. "Steven wants to be your *Gnecht* (farmhand), and Daed said he may. You surely won't need both a *Maad* (maid) and a *Gnecht*."

"Don't be too sure," Joe told her. "Before we can milk cows, we'll have to get that dairy barn in shape. I wouldn't be a bit surprised if we ask you to help prepare the food for the workers at the frolic. But that's a long way off yet, probably not before school lets out." He headed for the house.

Nancy sighed as she grabbed the calf buckets and hurried off to do her chores. Spring was a long way off yet. She could hardly wait to see the farm onto which Joe and Arie would be moving then.

Joe had told her that the farm had a name, a real name, painted on the side of the huge old stone bank barn: Chestnut Ridge Acres. It was a fitting name, for there was a ridge with chestnut trees growing on it. It was way back in the hills, and there was even a creek flowing through the meadow.

Nancy could hardly wait to explore the place. But she would have to wait until spring. Until then, Joe would live at home and spend his weekends with Arie at the Miller's farm, or the newly married pair would be visiting relatives together.

Susie came running from the house, carrying her barn boots. "Will Joe have to grow a beard then, too, like Jacob did after he was married?" she asked, panting as she slipped into her boots.

"Of course," Nancy told her. "Did you ever see an Amish man without a beard? Here, give this bucket of feed to Spot, and don't let him butt it over. We have to hurry this morning."

With Susie's help, Nancy's share of the chores was soon finished. They headed for the house with Dad, Omar, Steven, and Henry, who had milked the cows and fed the horses, pigs, and the rest of the livestock.

There was a beautiful sunrise with a rosy hue, and Dad commented, "Looks like it will be a fine day for Joe's wedding. Now, boys, be sure to mind your manners. You too, Susie," he said, tweaking her ear. "I won't have to worry about Nancy."

Nancy smiled gratefully. This was to be her first wedding at someone else's home, and she hoped she would know how to act. Mary's wedding had been right here at home, and that was different.

In a low voice so Dad wouldn't hear, Henry told Susie, "If you don't behave, the table waiters might stand you on your head and pour out the mischief, like they used to do years ago."

Susie stamped her foot. "They'd better not try it," she pouted. "Besides, I'm going to behave. Just watch that they don't try to throw you over a fence, Henry. That might settle your own mischief."

Joe came out of the house wearing his new plain-cut suit and broad-rimmed hat, ready to leave for Arie's home. With a wave of his hand, he untied Chief, climbed into the buggy, and was off, going out the lane.

This long-looked-for day had finally arrived. In a few hours, he and Arie would be married, for better or worse, richer or poorer, until death would part them. But with such a sweet, dependable girl like Arie for a *Fraa* (wife), Joe had no qualms about the future. They would be partners and best friends for life.

Joe found himself wishing that spring were already here so he and Arie could move to their farm right away. He wanted to prove that they could make a go of farming at Chestnut Ridge Acres. That was a challenge that appealed to Joe.

"C'mon Chief," he urged his horse on. "Let's go." Chief snorted, blowing puffs of steam out of his nostrils into the frosty air. He trotted fast and upheaded, prancing as if he knew that today was the day his master was to be married.

Joe began to sing *"das Lobleid* (the Praise Song)." He was happy, life was good, and the future looked rosy. Little did he realize the ups and downs that would come in their first year of marriage or even that first day.

2

Trapped

ARIE went to the window and peered out. Any minute now, she would see the familiar sight of Joe's Chief, trotting in the lane, and Joe, tall and manly, striding in the walk to her. He would be the first one there. Then the cooks would arrive to make the turkey roasts, and later the table waitresses and hostlers would roll in.

She looked around to see if there was anything else to do. The benches were set in place, and everything seemed to be in apple-pie order. Down in the cellar, temporary tables had been set up and were laden with food prepared for the wedding meal. There were twenty beautifully frosted cakes, plus the decorated wedding cake that was to be placed on the

Eck (corner) table where the bridal party would sit.

Crocks of pudding and fruit salad and tubs of cubed cheese were stashed there. Crisp, beautifully bleached celery had been washed and put in pans of shallow water. The freshly made filled doughnuts were on the shelf. In Arie's way of thinking, no Lancaster County Amish wedding would be complete without them.

Over one hundred pounds of potatoes had been peeled, ready to be cooked and made into *gschtammde Grummbiere* (mashed potatoes). The homemade noodles were ready to be tossed into boiling water, and the colorful chowchow was in jars on the shelf.

Arie was dressed in her wedding *Rock* (dress) she had made several months ago especially for this day. Her wavy dark brown hair was neatly combed back under her *Kapp* (prayer covering). Her cheeks were flushed from the excitement and flurry of getting ready. When Joe arrived and she hurried out to help him unhitch, he was sure that with her dimpled cheeks and big brown eyes, she was the prettiest girl he'd ever seen.

"How do you feel?" Joe asked Arie. "Nervous?"

Arie nodded. "Whatever you want to call it. I've got *Summerfliegles* (butterflies) in my middle. How about you?"

Joe shook his head and smiled. "I think I've got them in my heart, though, when I look at you."

Arie blushed. "We'd better go inside. The cooks will be here soon."

Almost before they realized it, the guests were ar-

15

riving. Hostlers took their horses and carriages and marked each rig with chalk so they could match families with their own horses and vehicles for the trip home. They parked the buggies and tied the horses.

Ushers stood at the doors, greeting the guests, taking their wraps, and receiving a few wedding presents. The bridal party was seated on the proper chairs. When the first hymn was announced, Joe and Arie followed the bishop and ministers upstairs to one of the rooms, to be instructed and counseled in the basics of Christian *Eheschtand* (marriage).

Downstairs, the melodious volume of singing filled the rooms, the old slow tunes rising like a sweet chorus, touching the families' and the guests' hearts with gladness. When the music drifted through the register to the counsel room above, Joe and Arie's hearts, too, were stirred with joy. It was humbling to realize that these special services were for them. Others would benefit, too, and renew and rededicate their lives to God.

After they came downstairs, the bishop preached the wedding sermon. Joe and Arie sat with bowed heads, listening to the impressive and meaningful words. Being joined in the bonds of holy matrimony was a solemn and sacred step.

When it was nearly time to make their vows as husband and wife, the bishop said, "Before us today we have Joe Petersheim and Arie Miller, a brother and sister in the faith who have agreed to enter the bonds of holy matrimony together. If anyone is present who can bring an objection and has a good reason why

these two cannot be married in the Lord, let them come forth and speak now."

Everything was quiet enough to hear a pin drop. No one stirred while the bishop waited a few seconds.

Then he said, "There being no objection, you may stand and present yourselves for marriage."

Joe and Arie answered the usual questions and promised to be faithful to each other for life. Then they joined right hands.

The bishop pronounced them husband and wife and prayed for God's blessings upon them. The couple was seated again. The services were closed with testimony from the other ministers and deacon, followed by prayer and the closing hymn.

The rest of the day passed quickly. There was the wedding feast, and then the dishwashing by the helpers. The afternoon was spent visiting and singing. Most of the older people went home and left the youth there to carry on.

At the supper table, the guests were kidding each other and having a lot of fun. Under cover of the hubbub, Joe whispered to Arie, "Let's try to outwit the buddies tonight. I heard the guys boasting that they were going to throw me over the fence. Like fun they will! I know of a good clean hiding place in the *Fruchtkammer* (granary). If I see them coming for me, I'll just disappear."

Arie giggled. "If I know you, you'll best them," she said. "I'm going to do my best not to step over a broom, either, even though I have to hide, too. I'd just love to outwit the girls, too."

She knew her girlfriends would try to thrust a broom in front of her to trick her into stepping over it as a new bride. Then they would cheer and say they had initiated her into being a wife. Every Amish bride watched carefully to keep this from happening, but the girls usually persisted until they succeeded.

After supper the young folks went out to the *Scheierdenn* (barn floor). It had been cleaned out in readiness for the evening, and the hostlers had hung lanterns from the beams so they would have light to play party games.

Joe and Arie watched awhile, then went back into the house. As the guests left, they came and shook hands with the newly married couple and wished them *gute Glick* (good luck) or the Lord's blessings.

Finally their buddies were about the only ones left. Arie happened to glance up just in time to see a broom being smuggled in through the washhouse door, behind the skirts of the girls. Joe saw it, too, and winked at her. Then, out of the corner of her eye, she saw the girls headed in their direction.

Arie quickly stepped back, went into the pantry, and wedged the ironing board against the door to hold it shut. An idea was forming in her mind. She opened the low window, climbed over the sill, and stepped out. Before she closed the window, she heard someone knocking on the pantry door and calling, "I saw you going in there, Arie, and I can wait as long as you can. Enjoy yourself in there."

Chuckling to herself, Arie sped around the house. Wouldn't it be great if she could trick her buddies! As she passed a window that had been pushed open for fresh air, she crouched low against the bushes. She heard one of the girls say loudly, "Do you know what Arie did? She locked herself in the pantry. The minute she walks out of there, she's going to step over the broom. She won't get the best of us."

Arie stifled a giggle and sped on. She looked up to see a cloud traveling in front of the moon and thought, *What a strange thing to be doing on my wedding night.* She opened the back hall door and ran lightly up the deserted stairs. The house was like most old farmhouses; there were two stairways, the main front stairway and the creaky, seldom-used back stairway.

"I'll baffle them for awhile," Arie exulted. She crossed the small storeroom that was closed off to the guests and opened the attic door. Near the top of the steps was the chest that had once been her mother's hope chest but now was empty except for a few pillows. It was a perfect hiding place, nice and clean and soft.

Arie climbed into the chest and carefully lowered the lid. Laughing to herself, she thought, *I'll wait until they're completely beat out. Then I'll go back down and laugh at them. But I won't step over their broom! Joe will be so tickled.*

She shifted her weight on the pillows to find the most comfortable position. Suddenly she heard a click. The lid had latched. Heart pounding, Arie tried to sit up and push open the lid. She pushed with all her might, but it was no use. She was trapped in the chest.

3

A Close Call

A feeling of awful doom enveloped Arie. Why hadn't she thought about the lid latching? How long would the oxygen last in this small place?

She wanted to scream and cry and pound on the lid, but she knew it wouldn't do a bit of good. The chest was heavy and solidly built, and she would only use up the oxygen faster. She pushed down her panic and tried to reason calmly, but tears ran from her eyes.

Thoughts raced through her mind. *What an awful way to die, especially on my wedding night! Will Joe think I ran away from him on purpose? Will I ever be found? Or will someone find my bones years from now?*

Arie shuddered. Was she ready to face the judgment seat of Christ? She was thankful that she had given her heart to the Lord and tried to obey him and had joined church. But she wanted to live and to serve God and do good for years and years yet.

More tears wet her cheeks. "Dear God," she prayed, "please send someone to rescue me before I die. In Jesus' name I pray. Amen." For a few moments, Arie felt a new calmness and lifting of her spirits. Surely God had the power to send someone to find her here before it was too late. But then her heart sank again. What if it wasn't God's will? What if her time to die had come?

Bravely she fought back her tears and declared, "If my time has come to die, then I will submit. God makes no mistakes." She relaxed and closed her eyes in the darkness. She would try to go to sleep quietly. Maybe she would die peacefully and wake up with the angels.

Arie closed her eyes in the darkness and willed herself to breathe slowly and deeply. She would not panic; she dare not panic. Suddenly Arie tensed, her heart beating fast with renewed hope. From far off and faintly, someone was calling, "Arie, Arie, where are you?"

For a long moment, Arie seemed to be petrified and unable to move. Then she sprang to action. "Help, help!" she cried, pounding on the lid with all her might. "Here I am, inside this chest."

She pounded again and again, but the voice seemed to become fainter and more muffled. Arie refused to give up hope. "Help, help!" she called again.

She took off her shoe and banged the heel against the lid, fast and hard. She shouted and pounded for what seemed to be a long time. But when she stopped to listen, all was deathly, unbearably quiet.

Arie was determined not to be trapped forever. She reminded herself that she was in a *hope* chest. Wildly and blindly, almost beside herself, she clawed at the clasp of the chest. Then, once again, she heard, "Arie, Arie, where are you?"

Muffled footsteps sounded across the attic floor, but they seemed to grow fainter and far away. "Arie, Arie!"

Arie tried to answer, but no sound came from her mouth. It was like being in a hazy dream She wanted to knock on the lid and answer, but nothing happened. She tried to struggle, but her arms would not obey.

Was it too late? No one would know where to find her now. She was blacking out. The voice seemed to be growing fainter again, but Arie didn't care anymore. She just wanted to rest.

The next moment someone opened the chest. Arie was only dimly aware that Dad was there with a lantern. Joe and others were with Dad. They lifted her up, carried her down the attic stairs, and placed her on a bed.

In a few minutes the fresh air had revived her. Arie sat up. "*Danki Gott* (thank God)," she murmured, smiling shakily. Seeing Joe's concerned face, she took his arm and got to her feet. "Let's go," she said. "I'm ready to step over that broom now."

The day after the wedding was a busy one, working to get things back in place. Joe loaded the benches back into the church's gray bench wagon and hauled it to the farm where the next wedding was to be held, on Thursday.

Arie was feeling fine again. Gratitude flooded her heart as she helped pack dishes into the chests. "Never again will I take life and health for granted," she resolved. "That surely felt like a close call." But she would never really know whether it was lack of oxygen or her emotions that made her faint.

Arie's mother came out of the pantry, carrying a stack of platters. "Did you decide already when you will leave for your visit to Summerville? Or weren't you able to round up a driver?"

"Friday morning, and we're going by train!" Arie exclaimed happily. "I'm so excited about it. I've never had a train ride before. We're going to visit Mary and Jacob. Then on Saturday we'd like to drive out to our farm and explore, and take a walk through the chestnut ridge. We start back again on Monday."

"I'm anxious to see your farm, too," her mom said. "Will you be able to tour the house, too, or is it still occupied?"

"It's still occupied. The present renters won't be leaving until the first of March," Arie told her. "But I'm hoping the lady of the house will invite me inside. I sure am anxious to see it."

"Will you have any close neighbors?" Mom wondered. Having good neighbors was a high priority she had for her daughter when she moved so far away.

She knew that moving into a new neighborhood without knowing anyone would not be easy.

"Just one cranky old man," Arie lamented. "At least that's what Joe thinks. He sure didn't seem friendly when Joe talked to him. Oh well, maybe I can bake a few pies for him, or somehow or other we can make a friend out of him."

After working hard all day, Joe and Arie decided to go for a stroll after supper to enjoy the beautiful evening. It had been a beautiful *Altweiwersummer* (Indian summer) day, and the sun was setting in a bank of rosy clouds in the west.

"We could walk hand in hand, or arm in arm, like the *Englisch* (non-Amish) do," Joe remarked, smiling teasingly.

Arie smiled back. "Too much audience," she said, chuckling. "What would the neighbors think? Just wait till we get up to the chestnut ridge. No one will see us there but one old man."

"That reminds me. I'd like to talk to the farm's owner tonight. The last I talked with him, he said there's a possibility he'll sell us the farm instead of just renting it to us. Let's stop at the phone shanty, and I'll place the call."

Arie waited outside while Joe went up the steps to the small wooden phone booth that several Amish neighbors shared. When he came back, he said jubilantly, "Good news! He's ready to sell, and the price is reasonable. That's just what Daed and I were hoping he'd say. That means we can put up a real dairy barn instead of trying to put the dairy into the old barn that isn't suitable at all."

"We'll do our best, won't we?" Arie said, her brown eyes shining. "I've fallen in love with the place already, even though I haven't seen it yet. But it wonders me so what the house is like."

"Whatever you don't like about it, we'll change it around someday to suit you," Joe promised. "We'll make it the farm of our dreams."

4

Scammed

AT the Lancaster train station on Friday morning, Joe and Arie bought their round-trip tickets and sat on a bench to wait for their train.

"I'm so excited!" Arie said eagerly. "First the train ride, then we'll see Mary and Jacob and Nancy Ann. Best of all, we'll get to look over our farm. I can hardly wait."

Joe chuckled at Arie's enthusiasm. "Don't get your expectations too high," he warned. "Remember, it isn't a well-kept Amish farm yet. Whoever had it last really let it go to the dogs. But it's nothing that can't be remedied with a lot of hard work."

"If the setting is as nice as you say it is, I'm not worried." Arie's spirits were undaunted, and she chatted happily on. "I wonder why not more of our people go to Summerville on the train. Going by train is much more exciting."

"Going by van is handier," Joe reminded her. "We would get picked up at home and taken right to the place we want to go. By train, we have to find a way to and from the station. But this is much nicer, especially for a honeymoon trip." He smiled at her.

Arie glowed in response. She had decided to forget about the unpleasant experience of being trapped in the chest. She would not let it cast a shadow over these special early days of their marriage. Surely nothing like that would ever happen to her again.

Looking around, she began to notice all the different people at the station. Some were quite decent looking, while others were unkempt and rough looking.

Arie's thoughts were interrupted by a voice over the loudspeaker, announcing their train.

"Let's go," Joe said, picking up the suitcase. They hurried down the steps to the outside walkway and watched as the Amtrak train came gliding to a stop. The doors opened and the young couple quickly boarded the train and found a seat.

"What luxury!" Arie exclaimed. "Plenty of room to stretch our legs, and even to recline our seats and snooze if we want to. Do you mind if I take the seat by the window?"

"Go ahead," Joe told her. "I'll protect you from those rough-looking guys that were ogling us there in the station."

Arie nodded. "They were probably only staring at my shawl and bonnet, or your broad-brimmed hat. Maybe they never saw Amish people before."

Joe nudged Arie and motioned to the next seat. The rough-looking men had taken the seat across the aisle from them.

Arie whispered, "I thought most teenagers had long hair nearly to their shoulders nowadays. Those guys have their heads partly shaved. Doesn't that look *unvergleichlich* (weird)?"

"It's a good thing they don't understand *Deitsch* (Pennsylvania German/Dutch)," Joe replied. "It must be a new fad. But I'm sure they think we look *unvergleichlich,* too."

Arie relaxed and sat looking out the window as the scenery flew by. She had been too excited to eat breakfast this morning, and now she was empty and thirsty.

"I wish I'd have thought to bring a jug of cider or a few sandwiches," she told Joe. "Do you think I'd be able to buy something here on the train?"

"Oh, yes, I'm sure we can. You have the wallet in your bag. There's a dining car somewhere. But here, let me go with you. I've been on this train once before, but not since I was about twelve years old. There's even a rest room here somewhere."

When they returned to their seats, Arie remarked, "A train ride sure is fun, isn't it?"

Joe nodded. "Did you know that when train travel first became common years ago, *unser Leit* (our people) thought it was too worldly and shunned 'the devil's contraption,' as they called it? Now we travel by train and think flying in a jet is too modern."

"Hmmm, that's interesting," Arie said. "Times sure change, even for us, don't they?"

The men across the aisle were talking to each other in low tones. Then, loud enough for Joe and Arie to hear, the one closest to Joe said, "I'm going to go get some chow."

He dug into his pocket for a handful of loose change. Something clinked loudly to the floor and rolled near Joe's seat. The man quickly went down on his hands and knees to hunt for it. "Where did that confounded coin go?" he muttered.

The other chap leaned over to help search "Maybe it's under the lady's seat," he suggested.

Joe got down on his knees, too, and helped to hunt for the lost money. "Move your feet a bit," he told Arie. "Maybe it's under your shoe."

Arie jumped up and helped in the search. But the missing coin wasn't to be found.

"I'm sorry," Joe said politely. "Maybe it rolled back under the next seat."

The guy searched about the surrounding seats but finally gave up. Swearing under his breath, he sat down.

"How much was it?" Joe asked. "We can give you a dollar if you're short of funds."

"Oh, no no!" The guy seemed alarmed and quickly got to his feet. "Here's where we get off anyway." They hurried to the front and stood waiting while the train slowed and came to a stop. As soon as the doors opened, they took off running.

"It seems to me there was something mighty suspicious about those chaps," Arie observed. "Why were they so alarmed when you offered to give them a dollar?"

"It sure beats me," Joe replied, shaking his head. "After the fuss they had over losing a few cents."

Suddenly Joe sat bolt upright in his seat. "Check the wallet!" he cried.

Arie reached in her bag and then looked dazed. "It's gone!"

Joe sprang from his seat and sprinted down the aisle.

"Wait, Joe!" Arie called in alarm. Was he going to run after the crooks and leave her alone on the train?

After what seemed like a long time, Joe came back. "I reported it, but I don't think they'll be able to get our wallet back," he lamented. "They could be blocks from here by now." He sat down dejectedly.

"How much money was in the wallet?" Arie asked. "I hope it wasn't much."

"About forty dollars. *Ach, Yammer* (oh, trouble), how are we going to get around and buy our food on the way home with no money?" Joe asked in exasperation. "*Es macht mich so bees* (it makes me so mad)."

"Maybe Jacob will loan you some. I'm sure he will," Arie said comfortingly. "Let's be thankful that it wasn't more, and that they didn't attack us."

"Do you still think traveling by train is better than by van?" Joe teased her. "Maybe it is the devil's contraption after all."

Arie shook her head sadly. "The old saying doesn't

hold true anymore. *Wann du net drauscht, du net zu draue* (if you don't trust others, you are not to be trusted). Nowadays a person can't be blamed if he doesn't trust others."

"*Ya* (yes), well, let's not let it spoil our trip," Joe said. "At least I learned a lesson. I don't think I'll be scammed again."

5

Surveying Chestnut Ridge

WHEN Joe and Arie got off the train, they walked the two blocks to the store parking lot to which Jacob had given them directions. Sure enough, there were Mary and Jacob and little Nancy Ann, with two horses hitched to the market wagon.

"*Wie geht's* (how do you do)?" Jacob and Mary said in unison, coming forward to shake hands.

"My, it's good to see you," Mary added. "We've been looking forward to this so much."

"It's good to see dear familiar faces again, after all those strangers," Arie said gratefully. "I don't like to be in a *Schtadt* (city)."

"Hop in and we'll go, then," Jacob said briskly. "It's all of a ten-mile drive, which will mean a late dinner. Mary has a goose a-roastin' in the oven."

The women sat on the backseat and the men on the front. Arie was glad for the chance to get to know Joe's sister better, and Mary likewise was looking forward to having a chat with her new sister-in-law.

Little Nancy Ann peeked shyly around her mother's shawl, knocking her little black bonnet askew. Arie smiled at her, and the baby quickly hid her face in the shawl.

"She's cute," Arie said. "I was hoping you'd bring her along to the wedding." Mary smiled. "We would have, but we have a neighbor girl, Sally Fisher, who loves to babysit. She offered to watch the baby that day. It was real handy for us, too."

Jacob said, "So you want to go see your farm tomorrow? What is it, Chestnut Tree Farm? We'll let you use King and the trottin' buggy."

"Chestnut Ridge Acres," Joe corrected him. "We'd like to walk out to the ridge, so we're hoping for another *Altweiwersummer* (Indian summer) day. The leaves aren't all down yet, so we should have some nice scenery."

He added wryly, "I really appreciate it that we can use King. We sure wouldn't have any money to pay a driver." He told Jacob and Mary about being scammed on the train.

Jacob whistled under his breath. "Ei yi yi! Whew, they sure pulled a fast one there, didn't they? Didn't you notice anything at all?"

Joe shook his head. "Nothing that made us suspicious. Of course, we were busy looking around for their lost coin. They must have reached in Arie's bag and stole the wallet while we were distracted."

"Ya, well, it was just *Geld* (money). I'll gladly give you what you need to get back home," Jacob offered. *"Es hett shlimmer kennt* (it could have been worse)."

"Gross Dank (many thanks)," Joe said, with feeling. "I hope those *Diewe* (thieves) will be caught and apprehended."

It was late when they reached the Yoder home, and Mary's dinner of stuffed goose, baked potatoes and scalloped corn seemed extra delicious. The rest of the day was spent visiting. In the evening Joe helped Jacob with the milking.

On Saturday morning, true to his word, Jacob hitched King to the trottin' buggy for Joe and Arie, and Mary packed a picnic lunch for them.

"I hope we can repay you sometime soon," Joe said gratefully. "This is real hospitality."

"We'll see to it that you do," Jacob teased.

"Danki (thanks), and good-bye," Arie called with a wave of her hand. "See you tonight."

King was impatient to go, and with flying gravel, they were off.

"My, this air feels chilly," Arie remarked. "I'm glad I have my gloves."

Joe tucked the carriage robes more securely about them. "The sun will warm us up soon," he said. "Jacob thinks we have about eight or ten miles to our farm. It spites me that it isn't closer. It would be nice if we could work together at planting and harvesting time."

"Oh, well, we'll have Steven to help us, and maybe even Nancy sometimes," Arie assured him. "I can help you in the fields sometimes, too. But, oh, I'm so anxious to see the house. I trust we'll be allowed to see the inside of it. It wonders me so what kind of a kitchen I'll have."

She spoke dreamily, and Joe, glancing at his shining-eyed bride, hoped with all his heart that she would be pleased. He felt responsible for her happiness. What would he do if she didn't like the house?

King was feeling his oats, frisky and raring to go. Joe kept a tight grip on the reins as up and down the hills they went, then on to level countryside.

"This looks like nice farmland," Arie commented. "But I wonder why some of these farms look so dilapidated. The owners must not care."

Joe nodded. "I think it's because so often the young people have no interest in farming. They want an easier lifestyle, so they take off for the cities. The old people get tired and let the farms run down, and then we Amish can come in and buy them. In a few years, with good care, the farms will look prosperous again."

King kept up his swift pace, and the miles flew by, with Joe and Arie enjoying the interesting scenery. "We should be there soon," Joe said. "Just another half mile or so."

They drove into a hollow, and just ahead was a small bridge over a rushing, rocky stream.

"Oh, how beautiful," Arie breathed. "It's the most scenic spot I've ever seen."

King slowed, eyed the bridge warily, and stopped altogether. The bridge had no sides or guard rails of any kind. It was just a narrow slab of concrete from bank to bank.

"My, that's narrow," Arie gasped. "I think I'll walk across, if you don't mind." She got off the buggy and stood beside it, waiting to see what Joe would do.

"It is narrow," Joe agreed, in a concerned voice. "It sure wasn't made for a horse and buggy. If the horse shies from one side, he'll be down on the other side."

The bridge was not high, nor the stream deep. But if the buggy plunged over the side, it would turn over.

Joe got out too. "I think I'll try to lead King across." He took hold of the horse's bridle and tugged him forward. King snorted and pranced a bit, but refused to cross.

"He's too smart," Arie laughed.

Joe shook his head. "If he would be a little smarter, he'd quietly walk over the middle of the bridge. C'mon, King, try it," he urged.

However, King would not budge. Instead, he began to go backward.

"Might as well unhitch," Joe decided. "At least the buggy won't overturn then."

King wouldn't even walk over the bridge that way. Joe finally took off his shoes and socks, rolled up his pant legs, and led him through the water and up to the road on the other side. Arie pulled the buggy over the bridge by the shafts, and in a few minutes they had King hitched again. Joe dried his feet on the carriage robe and put on his socks and shoes.

"I sure hope you won't get pneumonia from that cold water," Arie worried. "Aren't you just chilled to the bone?"

"Nah, I don't think I'll mind it," Joe shrugged it off. "When Daed was a boy, they used to go barefooted from April to November, to save their shoes. So I hope I'm not that much of a cream puff that I can't stand a bit of wading.

"Say, what if other people's horses mind that bridge as much as King does and won't cross it? We can't expect many of *unser Leit* (our people) to visit us if their horses won't cross that bridge. There's no other road to our farm. Maybe we can get some help and widen the bridge."

"My, look at all those squirrels scampering up and down the trees," Arie marveled. "I'm sure that in summertime there would be lots of nice birds around here, too. This sure is back country."

"Did you hear that pheasant crowing?" Joe asked. "That's music to my ears. This area is still rich in wildlife. Back home, the wild animals are getting so scarce that it's hardly worthwhile going out for small game."

Before long Joe pointed up the hill toward some buildings. "Oh, look, there you can see our farm!"

Arie sat gazing, taking in the scene with a smile on her lips. "It's a beautiful setting," she exclaimed in delight. "Both the barn and the house are made of sandstone, and the chestnut ridge is *schee* (pretty) even with a lot of the leaves off the trees.

"Oh, Joe, drive faster! It looks *wunderbaar* (wonderful) from here, but I can't wait to see it closer."

Joe chuckled at Arie's excitement as he loosened the reins. They headed up the long winding lane at a fast trot. Arie's eyes took in everything as Joe tied King.

"I see that it will take a lot of cleaning up around here," she noticed. "Twigs and leaves are cluttering the yard, and look how the flower beds are overgrown with weeds."

"And there's a lot of junk between the house and the barn, too," Joe muttered. "It's a good thing the buildings can't be seen from the road."

"This *Marasch* (mess) won't be hard to remedy, come spring," Arie said optimistically. "With a few weeks of hard work after we move in, our place will sure look a lot better."

"I do like these nice big trees in the yard," responded Joe.

"Now if only we'd be able to tour the house yet," Arie added. "I'm just bursting with curiosity. And it would be nice to let it warm up a bit before we walk back to the chestnut ridge, especially with your cold feet.

"Oh, look," she added, pointing to the barn. "There's the name, CHESTNUT RIDGE ACRES. Its paint is so faded that I didn't notice it before."

"Once we get settled and have time, I'll paint that barn," said Joe. "Then I'll have to paint over the sign so our people don't think we're proud. But we can still call our farm Chestnut Ridge Acres. It'll be fun to get this place a bit more presentable for visitors."

"Oh, I can just hardly wait until spring," Arie said enthusiastically. "I'm so eager to move here."

"Whoa, King," Joe said as they stopped by the yard fence. He tied King to the post.

Arie climbed out of the buggy. "I sure wonder what the house is like. I hope there's a big kitchen. Let's ask to look through the house first, before we check the barn."

"Yes, we'll do that," replied Joe. He wanted his wife to be happy in this move, but now he was just a bit uneasy.

6

Droppings in the Buggy

WHEN Joe and Arie knocked on the kitchen door of the farmhouse, they were pleasantly surprised by the warm welcome the lady of the house gave them.

"Hello, come in," she invited them cordially. "So you'll be the next occupants of this house. I'm sure you're anxious to see it, then. You're welcome to inspect all the rooms."

She led them into the kitchen first, and Arie's heart sank a bit when she saw it. It was small, with only one window, and the kitchen cabinets could not have been more than four feet wide. The linoleum was worn through at places, and the walls were uneven and sloppily painted.

So much for my dream kitchen, she thought ruefully. She had envisioned a big airy, sunshiny kitchen with old-fashioned oak cabinets forming an L shape, plenty of windows, and room for their settee and homemade rugs and Joe's desk. This dark little room lacked cheer and homey warmth.

Oh, well, maybe the other rooms would make up for it. Bravely she swallowed her disappointment. The lady let them explore the house on their own and went back to her work. Much to Arie's disappointment, the other rooms were also small and poorly designed. A big hall ran through the center of the house.

Joe said, "Maybe in a few years we can knock out some of these walls and put in folding doors so we can have church services in here. Till then, we'll probably have to meet in the barn."

Arie nodded her head. There was an unexpected lump in her throat, and she didn't quite trust herself to speak just then. She was ashamed of herself for feeling that way. Arie had her hopes so high, and now they were dashed. Could she make herself at home here?

Joe sensed her mood. Putting an arm around her, he said, "If everything goes as planned, in a few years we'll be able to make everything just like you want it. Do you think you can make out with it like this until then?"

Arie nodded and smiled. "I guess so. I'll have to think of how the pioneer women had things when they went out West in covered wagons. They sometimes had to live in sod houses and claim shanties and crude log cabins. Many of them didn't see their families again for years and sometimes never again.

"I'll try to make it cheerful and livable here," she promised. "It could be a lot worse. We'll make it 'Home, Sweet Home.'"

Joe wanted to hug Arie, but just then the lady of the house returned.

"There's one room upstairs, the dog room, that I never set foot inside," she admitted. "You may go in if you want to, but I doubt that you will. I keep the door locked. Here's the key in case you want to look in. It's the room at the end of the hall. It's apparently where the previous renter's dogs lived, and I sure wasn't going to clean it out."

Joe and Arie went up the creaky stairs. "My curiosity is aroused," Arie declared. "Let's look at the dog room first."

"It might be bad," Joe warned her. "Are you sure you want to open the door? Maybe we shouldn't."

"It won't hurt to look," Arie suggested. "I want to know."

Joe inserted the key in the lock and slowly opened the door.

"*Ach, du lieber* (oh, my goodness)!" Arie exclaimed. She gulped, stepped back, and covered her nose with her handkerchief.

Joe quickly shut the door and locked it again. "Phew!" He got out his handkerchief too. "*Ach, mei Zeit* (oh, my, my)! How can that woman stand living with such a room in the house? Ugh!"

"Let's get out of here," Arie whispered. "This is awful! I think I could cry." And she was close to tears.

43

They managed to thank the lady for letting them see the house, and then quickly went out into the bright November sunshine. The lady followed them to the door, and Joe asked her, "Is it all right if we explore the farm and fields yet? We have a picnic lunch along."

"Oh, sure, go ahead," she answered. "Just don't bother the old man, Old Capp Griggs, who lives in the ramshackle old house by the woods just west of here. He's mighty cantankerous and crabby, and he might make trouble for you," she warned them. "He has a vicious old cur of a dog, too."

"Okay, we'll be careful," Joe promised. "Thanks again for showing us the house."

She went back into the house, and Arie said to Joe, "I want to wash my hands somewhere. I feel awful dirty."

Joe chuckled. "That's your imagination," he told her. "But I feel the same way. Here's the water trough by the barn."

There was a clear stream of spring water running from the old spigot. Arie scrubbed her hands for a long time and wished for soap. How could she ever live in that house?

"Let's forget about the dog room," Joe advised her. "We'll have plenty of help to clean that out. I'll make sure that it will be done before you see it again, so don't worry about it."

Arie wished she could forget it. But how could she ever forget such a sickening scene?

Joe was untying King. "Let's drive back the field

lane close to the ridge and then walk the rest of the way," he suggested. "We can tie King to a fence or a tree."

"At least it has warmed up." Arie tried to be cheerful. "It feels like Indian summer again."

"Just right for a picnic," Joe said brightly, matching her mood.

King pranced briskly along the rutted field lane. The bright sunshine, falling leaves, and chattering squirrels lifted their spirits.

"I'm so glad it's a nice day," Arie said thankfully. "It's so beautiful back here."

"Look, there's Old Capp's house." Joe pointed out the shabby little house that was more like a shack, just west of them. Behind the house were a rickety old barn and a dilapidated shed.

"Are you sure we're not on his land?" Arie asked a bit nervously. "It seems rather close."

"I don't think so, though I'm not sure yet where the property line is," Joe answered. "I'm quite sure the ridge belongs to our farm, though."

"I wonder what makes him so bitter and crabby," Arie mused. "Maybe we can win him over with kindness and being neighborly. Poor old man, living in that rough shack all alone. I pity him."

The field lane was uphill now, and the going got hard for King. So Joe turned him off the path and tied him to a sapling. "It's so gorgeous back here," Arie said rapturously. "Whenever we're feeling blue, we can come back here and go home cheered up. "

"If we're not too busy," Joe reminded her. He didn't

want to say it aloud, but he had a feeling they would really have their hands full for a while. There was so much work to be done.

Joe and Arie hiked up the trail, carrying the picnic lunch, breathing in the crisp, fresh air, and enjoying the scenery. A bunny bounded away from them lickety-split, with white tail bobbing. Pheasants crowed, squirrels chattered, and chickadees, nuthatches, and woodpeckers were frequently seen and heard. A tiny chipmunk with fat cheeks ran over a log and disappeared under it.

"The stream that you led King across has to be here somewhere," Arie declared. "It flows through the meadow, doesn't it?"

"Yes, over on the other side of the ridge we'll see it," Joe told her. "It winds around that way. Look at all these acorns and shellbarks (hickory nuts). It's a pity that these will all go to waste. Next year we'll gather them."

"They won't go to waste," Arie chuckled. "Not if these bushy-tailed fellows can help it."

She stopped and peered at the ground. "What kind of tracks are these?" she asked, puzzled. "They're almost big enough to be horse's tracks."

Joe examined the tracks in the soft earth. "Why, these are bear tracks!" he exclaimed excitedly. "I didn't know there are bears in this area."

"Bears!" Arie's eyes widened. "What if we meet one up here?" She looked over her shoulder nervously.

"Don't worry," Joe told her comfortingly. "I'm sure the bears in this area are almost as scarce as hens'

teeth, and besides, a bear would probably be more afraid of us than we of him."

They strolled on, then paused. Arie gasped softly, "Ach, just look at that!" Not more than a hundred feet away, a big buck had stepped into a clearing. He stood poised for a few moments, then away he bounded, with a flip of his tail.

"This is really getting exciting," Joe said in admiration. "What will we see next?"

They were on a trail winding down the other side of the ridge. Nestled at the bottom was a pond where ducks and geese were swimming. Among them was a pair of hooded mergansers with white tufts on their heads.

"It's so beautiful," Arie kept saying, as she gazed down over the valley.

"This makes up for the dog room, doesn't it?" Joe said, grinning. "We could build ourselves a cabin back here if that room bothers you too much."

"Don't mention it," Arie protested. "I was just starting to get hungry for the picnic lunch."

After another half hour of hiking, Arie's appetite had returned, and they sat on a rock ledge overlooking their farm to eat their lunch. After they had eaten, they still lingered, talking, dreaming, and planning.

A turkey gobbler and two hens passed cautiously by in the field below. "What a hunter's paradise!" Joe remarked. "Steven will really love this. He's a born outdoorsman."

He got up and stretched. "Ya, well, I guess we should soon be on our way. King must be getting hungry, too. I have some oats and hay along for him, and I'd like to explore the barn again, too."

When they neared the rig, Arie spied a figure walking across the field toward the old man's buildings, with a dog at his side.

"Do you think that's Old Capp?" she wondered.

"Sure is," Joe declared. "That's old Pappy Capp. I can recognize him by his gait. He's carrying a shovel. I wonder what he was up to."

They didn't have to wait long to find out. There was a rock on the buggy seat with a paper under it. It was a note, scrawled in crude handwriting, warning them to stay off his land. Joe began to laugh uproariously when he saw what else Capp had done.

"Just look what he did." He pointed to the floor of the buggy. Old Capp had shoveled a big pile of the horse's droppings into it.

Arie began to laugh, too, in spite of herself. "At least he was polite enough not to put them on the seat," she said, chuckling. "We could go thank him for that and ask to borrow his shovel in the bargain."

"Let's not forget to ask him if he wants some free fertilizer," Joe added. "Return good for evil, you know."

Arie laughed at Joe's joke. But she secretly resolved somehow or other to win the poor old man over to friendship, even if it took her many a month to do it. Surely there was a soft spot somewhere deep in his heart that would respond to kindness.

7

Moving In

THE winter months passed quickly with Joe and Arie making their rounds to the relatives nearly every weekend for meals, visiting, staying for the night, and collecting wedding presents. They were happy, but longing for spring, when they could move to Chestnut Ridge Acres and set up house-keeping.

Arie's thoughts often turned to Old Capp, alone there in his shack, with the deep winter snows piled around it. She wondered if his shabby house was warm and whether he had enough to eat. Was he lonely and unhappy?

During the week, Joe and his dad attended every farm sale within range, buying the necessary farm equipment, workhorses, and a cow, which would be trucked out to the farm in the spring.

Arie and her mother also went to household sales, buying what was necessary to begin housekeeping. Arie's uncle was a skilled furniture maker, so she had placed an order with him. He was crafting a new bedroom suite, a fourteen-foot table, twelve chairs, a hutch, a settee and a rocker to match, and a bench. The rest they would buy secondhand.

From his parents, Joe would receive a Windsor desk, a bedroom suite, and a beautiful handmade patchwork quilt. Joe and Arie were eagerly awaiting the spring, when they could move into their own home and use all the things they had carefully gathered.

The first day of spring finally arrived. A week later was moving day, on a Saturday. Mary had written them a letter, telling them that the Summerville Amish women were planning to get together, as soon as the previous renters moved out. They would clean the house from top to bottom, including the dog room. But still Arie was worried. Did they know how bad it really was? Maybe they just decided to nail the door shut. She sure pitied them, with a job like that.

On moving day, the stars were still shining when Joe and Arie got into the front seat of the furniture truck with the driver. To get an early start, the family loaded the household goods the day before. Arie's parents and most of Joe's family were going by van.

Another large truck with a horse trailer would follow them. It was taking the farm equipment, the horses, and one milk cow, to keep them in milk until they built their new barn and set up their dairy. That truck was loaded the previous evening. Joe's brothers Omar and Steven helped the truck driver coax the animals into the trailer early that morning. The two boys would ride along in that truck.

It was going to be a busy, eventful day. Arie tried to relax as the miles sped by. Sometimes she felt as if she ought to pinch herself to see if it was real. Were they really ready to begin housekeeping, so far away from their parents and families? What if she'd get a terrible case of *Heemweh* (homesickness)? *I won't get homesick, no matter what,* she told herself firmly.

As if able to read her thoughts, Joe asked, "Do you think you'll be able to survive with only an odd old man for a neighbor? Maybe we should have brought one of your nieces along, to keep you company when I am out in the fields."

Arie confidently replied, "Oh, no, I'll be all right. If I get homesick, I'll help you in the field. I'm used to driving the horses and helping Dad with the field-work."

She thought, *If I do get homesick, I'll make sure Joe won't find it out, nor anyone else.*

When they came to the narrow bridge near Chestnut Ridge Acres, the driver said, "Aha, what have we here?" He got out and measured the bridge with his tape measure, and then checked the span of the wheels. "It'll be close enough, but I think we'll make it," he told them.

Arie held her breath while he slowly inched the

truck, across. She breathed a sigh of relief when they were safely over. And then, there it was, the dear old farm on the Chestnut Ridge!

When they hopped out of the truck, Jacob was there to greet them. They were glad for the chance to stretch their legs. Joe saw Jacob's *Dachwegli* (carriage) in the barnyard, and right away he asked, "I'd like to know how you got King across that bridge."

Jacob laughed. "Ach, that was easy. I just blindfolded him and led him across."

Arie ran to the house. The van load of family was already there.

Mary met her at the door. "Come right in," she welcomed her. "We're at home."

Arie looked around and exclaimed, "Well, you dear folks did a *wunderbar* (wonderful) job! The house is clean! It makes the biggest difference."

"Come upstairs," Mary invited. "I want you to see the dog room."

Upstairs, Arie could hardly believe her eyes. The room that had been so repulsive was spotlessly clean and smelling of fresh paint and pine oil! "How did you ever get all those piles of dried-up dirt off the floor?" she asked in amazement. "You must have worked for more than one day."

"It wasn't so hard," Mary told her. "The men took out the old linoleum and pulled off the old wallpaper. After we cleaned it, they repainted the whole thing."

Arie was in a daze. She could hardly believe that it was the same room.

The truck with the farm machinery, the cow, and

the horses arrived, too. Everyone was soon busy. Some were at the barn, unloading the animals and machinery. Others were carrying furniture and household goods into the house.

Arie's head soon felt as if it were whirling, with everyone asking her where she wanted this or that. The stove was set up in the little kitchen. The dishes were unpacked, washed, and put into the cupboards. Furniture was put in place.

Arie put her red-checked oilcloth on the table and her cookie jar on top of the gas refrigerator. She shined the warming closet on the stove. Then she stepped back to take in the scene. She couldn't believe how cheery and cozy the little kitchen was after all.

Mary had brought a huge picnic basket of sandwiches for lunch. They were ready to rest a little after the unloading work. In the afternoon, the drivers left in their trucks, but the van load of family stayed for a few more hours to help finish unpacking and to organize things. Joe's dad helped him do some more planning on how to build the dairy barn.

In the evening when everyone had left, Arie sank into the rocker to rest her tired bones. Joe came in from feeding the horses and milking the cow. He pulled a chair up to the stove to warm his feet and asked, "Well, how do you feel?"

"Tired but happy!" she replied. "It's so nice to have our own place."

"Same here," Joe said. "Let's get to bed early. This district has church services tomorrow, and we have five or six miles to go. We don't want to be late the first time."

Later, snuggled in bed, Arie felt nearly overwhelmed by it all. Were they really in their own home and their own bed at last? It was nearly too good to be true, too much to comprehend.

She drifted off to sleep, sweet dreams drifting through her mind. How long they had slept, she didn't know, but suddenly they were awakened by loud clanging noises. They heard the banging of metal on metal, the roar of a chain saw, and the boing of a hammer on tin.

Joe and Arie sat up in bed, startled and confused. Then it dawned on them. The Amish youths of Summerville had come to *glabber* (serenade) them.

"We'd better get up and get dressed," Joe said. "They won't quit it until we open the door and let them in and treat them with something to eat."

"My, such a clanging and clamoring! It sounds like they're putting off firecrackers, too," Arie exclaimed. "What a racket!"

Joe lit the gas lamp in the kitchen. "Do you have enough on hand to feed them, and something to drink? They won't stop until we invite them in."

"I think so. I have the tub of cookies that Mom gave, and I'll make coffee." Arie went to the cupboard while Joe opened the door and called the *Yunge* (youths) in. My, what a relief it was to have that racket stopped!

They were a merry, lively bunch and came trooping in, more intent on making Joe and Arie feel welcome than on mischief. When they all had left again,

Arie looked at the clock. *"Mei Zeit* (my, my), it's one o'clock already!" she exclaimed. "How did the time go so fast? Next we'll oversleep and be late for church."

The next morning Joe hurried with his few chores in the old barn, and Arie quickly fried some mush and eggs. After breakfast they hurriedly dressed in their Sunday-best clothes. Joe hitched Chief to the carriage. They didn't think of the bridge until they were out the lane and on the road.

"Ach, Elend (oh, misery)!" Joe muttered. "Now I'll probably have to wade the creek again. We forgot a cloth to blindfold Chief."

"Maybe we could use my shawl," Arie offered. "That would do the job."

To their relief, Chief approached the bridge without a trace of fear and calmly trotted across.

"He must have more sense than King," Arie said, laughing. "Maybe he heard us saying we're afraid we'll be late for church."

"He's a good horse," Joe said fondly. "I wouldn't trade him for any other."

When they arrived at the farm where church services were to be held, no other teams were in sight.

"I can't understand this," Joe said, genuinely puzzled. "It must be close to eight o'clock already. Maybe I got my directions wrong. Let's drive in at least and ask where church is. That is, if there's anybody at home."

"There are children at the windows," Arie noticed. "And there comes the farmer."

"Wie geht's (how are you)?" the man asked, shaking hands. "My, you're early."

"Early?" Joe looked at Arie in bewilderment. "How can that be?"

"Yes, it's not seven o'clock yet. Next you would've caught us at the breakfast table yet."

"But we started off just after seven o'clock," Arie said, feeling as bewildered as Joe.

Suddenly Joe began to laugh. "I think I know what happened. One of those fellows who came to *glabber* us last night was tinkering with our clock. He must have turned it one hour ahead. I didn't notice it then, but now we're an hour early!"

"What a joke on us," Arie laughed. "Ach, well, that's better than being an hour late, isn't it?"

"It sure is," the man said, laughing heartily. "Ya, well, just come in and make yourselves at home."

Secretly, Arie was glad that they were early. Now she could watch the people arrive. She was looking forward to getting to know these people and hoped she would soon feel at home with this church group.

She thought it would have been so nice if Mary and Jacob had been with this church group, but they were in a neighboring district. However, Arie knew that the people here would do their best to make them feel welcome and at home.

8

Sabbath Breakers

THE next few weeks were busy ones for Joe and Arie. As soon as school was out, Dad would have more help at home, and Steven would arrive to help them. But the land was fit to plow *now*. As Joe had predicted, he put in long days in the fields. When he came in for supper, he was rather tired.

After supper, Arie would often go out to the barn and help Joe milk the cow, one on each side. The cow was gentle and used to being milked by either or both of them. As they milked, they would share the day's happenings and their dreams for the future. Then Arie would take the milk to the house while Joe finished feeding and bedding the animals with straw for the night.

Arie had been used to a remodeled frame house and had a hard time adjusting to the old stone farmhouse on Chestnut Ridge Acres. The mice seemed to have free roaming, and though she admitted it to no one, Arie was awfully afraid of mice.

Joe baited and set the traps every morning. They were snapped soon after he was out the door. Arie either had to carry them out herself or live with it till dinnertime (noon). After dinner, he set the traps again before he left for the fields.

It wasn't just the mice. Thousand-leggers also appeared in the sink and bathtubs regularly. And the spiders—she had to wage a constant war on spiders, and she was afraid of spiders, too.

In the middle of the first week, Arie had her first attack of homesickness. It was a chilly, gray, and cloudy day. Arie was battling a head cold and couldn't work outside. She was lonely, and by midafternoon it became acute.

"If only I could call my mother or one of my sisters on the telephone," she moaned. She struggled to keep back the tears, but it was no use. She had a dreadful case of *Heemweh* (homesickness), and she wept until her eyes and nose were red.

"I simply must stop acting like a baby," she scolded herself. Arie went to the mirror above the washbowl and had to laugh in spite of herself. What a sight she was!

A movement outside the window caught her eye. Was that Joe coming in from the field in the middle of the afternoon? *"Ach, Yammer* (oh, trouble), he can't

59

see me like this!" Arie gasped. "What, oh, what shall I do?"

The onions! She flew to the cellarway door, grabbed the bowl of onions from the shelf, and quickly began to peel them as fast as her fingers would fly. Joe might think the onions had made her cry. He must not know that she had *Heemweh*.

The door opened, and Joe walked over to her side. "What's wrong, Arie?" he asked, sounding concerned.

"I—I'm peeling onions," she said lamely. "I'll be all right soon."

Joe looked at her strangely. "What are you planning to make with the onions?"

"I—I'm going to make macaroni salad." She had decided it just that moment, though she felt bad about being so deceptive.

Joe put his arm around Arie. "Are you sorry you married me?" he asked softly. "Do you wish we had never moved to Chestnut Ridge Acres?"

Arie got her handkerchief out of her pocket and blew her nose. "Of course not," she declared. "I was just lonely in here without you."

She smiled through her tears. When Joe kissed her tenderly, she was happy again, and her *Heemweh* disappeared as if by magic.

"I need to go to town for some implement parts," Joe said. "Do you want to go with me?"

"Oh, yes, I need some groceries, too." Arie was glad for the chance and thought a change of scene would do her good. She quickly got ready while Joe hitched Chief to the buggy.

Out on the road, they met Capp and his surly-look-ing dog, out walking. He scowled and swung his fist in their direction as they passed.

"Ach, Yammer, I wonder what makes him so angry," Arie commented. "Something must have hap-pened to him sometime or other. Who could we ask about him?"

"I'll ask the storekeeper in town if I don't forget," Joe offered. "It's just a small town and probably every-one knows each other."

"My, this is a small town," Arie remarked as they drove into the parking lot at the hardware store. It's really just a little village."

"Ach, my," Joe muttered. "There's no tie railing here. How can we tie Chief? They must not have many Amish shopping here. What will we do?"

"I'll stay here and hold the reins while you get the parts you need," Arie offered. "Then you can stay with the horse while I get what I need."

Thus they managed. Inside the grocery store, Arie asked for a dozen oranges.

"I'm sorry," the clerk replied, "we don't have any today. Let's see, this is Tuesday. They won't be in be-fore Friday."

"That's all right," Arie said politely. "I'll just get ba-nanas instead."

Hmmm, she mused. *I must be all mixed up. I thought today was Wednesday.*

Arie gazed around the homey, old-fashioned store. There were barrels of potatoes and apples alongside hoes and shovels. Clear glass canisters held all kinds of candy. On the shelves were dried beans and brown rice in bulk containers, and jars of homemade jelly.

The storekeeper was a pleasant-looking elderly lady with a friendly smile and graying hair.

"I'll love to do my shopping here," Arie murmured happily to herself. "It's much homier and friendlier than a modern supermarket."

Joe was patiently waiting for her. When Arie climbed up on the buggy seat beside him, he said, "Well, I believe I found out what Old Capp's grudge is all about. I asked the hardware store clerk, and he knew all about it.

"About ten years ago, Capp and the owners of the Chestnut Ridge Acres had a battle royal over a boundary line. The sheriff was called in, and the case was settled, but Capp lost. He's been bitter about it ever since. He used to have a wife, too, but she just up and disappeared one day. No one knows where she went."

Arie shuddered. "Isn't that awful, nursing a grudge that long and refusing to forgive? He's doing himself a lot of damage. I sure pity him. But there's not much anyone can do as long as he's not willing to forgive. It's just too bad."

The rest of the week went much better for Arie. She could hardly believe that she had suffered a bout of *Heemweh*. Housekeeping was great, and she helped Joe in the fields whenever the ground was fit.

On Friday morning it was drizzling. The skies were overcast, and it looked for more rain. At the breakfast table Arie announced, "I'm going to wait till Saturday to do the laundry, in hopes that it'll be a better drying day."

Joe got a strange look on his face, then grinned. "I guess I was a little mixed up," he said sheepishly. "I thought today *was* Saturday."

Arie laughed with him. "I was mixed up, too, this week," she admitted. "It can easily happen when we're isolated from everyone else. The clerk at the grocery store set me straight."

Saturday morning dawned clear and windy. Joe started the wringer washer engine for Arie, and she got the laundry out early. It had cleared off without raining more than a few sprinkles, so Joe went to the fields to plow.

"I have a busy day ahead of me," Arie told herself. "There's the baking and cleaning to do, and I want to help Joe as soon as that's done."

She paused at the washhouse door and looked out. From high up in the backyard cherry tree, a robin burst into song. Its sweet, joyous trilling gladdened Arie's heart. "Ah, springtime," she murmured. "My favorite time of year. It's such a lovely day. I wish it were Sunday so we could go for a walk back to the chestnut ridge. It must be beautiful back there in the springtime."

Joe plowed all forenoon while Arie was busy making *Schnitzboi* (dried-apple pie) and sugar cookies. At dinnertime, Joe came in the door with a bouquet of silvery, velvet-like pussy willows for his wife.

"I figured you'd be longing for a token of springtime," he said shyly.

Happy and with shining eyes, Arie took the flowers and put them into a vase. "Ah, this, and heaven, too," she murmured.

Joe was amply rewarded. He hoped he would never again have to see his wife sad, with tears in her eyes.

When dinner was over, Joe let the horses rest a while longer and then went back to his plowing. Arie began cleaning the kitchen. The wash was flapping merrily in the breeze. As soon as the kitchen was cleaned, she wanted to bring the clothes in and fold them.

After scrubbing the kitchen floor, she flung the bucket of dirty water out the door. Just then she spied a horse and *Dachwegli* (carriage) come driving in the lane.

"Oh, good! Visitors!" Arie exclaimed happily. "Just what we need."

It was Mary and Jacob and little Nancy Ann.

"*Kumm rei, kumm rei* (come in)," Arie welcomed Mary eagerly at the door. "I just finished cleaning my kitchen. Oh, it's so good to see you."

Suddenly she noticed that Mary wasn't smiling. There was a strange look on her face.

"Why, *was is letz* (what's wrong), Mary?" she asked in alarm. "Is something the matter?"

"Ah—er—not really," Mary stammered. "But it's—ah—we were at church this forenoon."

"At church?" Arie echoed. "What church? Was there a funeral? Today's Saturday."

Mary shook her head. "No, it's Sunday." Then she

burst out laughing. She sat down on a chair and laughed till the tears came, and Arie laughed with her.

Meanwhile, Jacob walked out to the field to meet Joe at the end of the furrow he was plowing. He couldn't understand this. Was Joe so busy that he had to work on a Sunday, or was he *ab im Kopp* (off in the head)?

Joe stopped the horses and came forward to meet Jacob, smiling broadly in welcome.

"*Wie geht's* (how are you), Jacob?"

Jacob shook hands with his brother-in-law. "It's a nice day for plowing, isn't it?"

"It sure is," Joe responded. "What brings you over here on a Saturday afternoon in your Sunday suit? If you'd have come in your everyday clothes, I'd have put you to work."

Jacob shook his head. "Ei yi yi," he said weakly. "I hate to tell you this, Joe, but this is Sunday. We were at church this morning."

Joe was stunned. "*Unvergleichlich* (strange)," he muttered. "*Unvergleichlich.*"

Jacob began to laugh. "Don't feel bad," he comforted. "Such things happen to the best of people. If you never make a worse mistake than this, you'll do all right."

Eventually Joe saw the humor of the situation, too, as Arie also finally had, and got a good laugh out of it. "Might as well put the horses away and change into Sunday clothes," he said sheepishly. "Just make sure you don't tell anyone about this. It's one of our most embarrassing moments."

"That I won't promise," Jacob teased. "It might be just too good not to tell it sometime. But I'll sit on it for now."

After Jacob and Mary had left for home, Arie meekly apologized to Joe for having misled him. "*Es dutt mir leed* (I'm so sorry), Joe. I guess we'll have to mark an *X* on the calendar for every passing day, so it doesn't happen again. Here by ourselves, we're like Robinson Crusoe on his island. He had to notch a stick to keep track of time."

"Let's not feel too bad about it," Joe responded. "It wasn't your fault any more than mine. We did give Jacob and Mary a good laugh. But I do wonder what Old Capp thought of these Amish people that work on Sunday. I saw him standing by his barn more than once today, just watching me. I wouldn't be surprised if his mouth was hanging wide open."

Arie had to laugh at the picture. "*Der Herr* (the Lord) knows we didn't do it on purpose. Maybe sometime we can tell Capp, too. We don't want to be a bad example for him."

"I'm thankful that it happened on our no church Sunday," Joe remarked. "If we'd have missed church, everyone would have wondered what was wrong. This way, maybe not many people will find it out. If Jacob keeps his tongue, that is."

"Hmmm," Arie replied, sagely, "don't count on that."

9

Angry Man,
Angry Dog

"I BELIEVE spring is really here to stay at last," Arie remarked happily to Joe at the breakfast table on Monday morning. "Just listen to that chorus of birds, singing outside. It seems like the robins and cardinals are trying to outdo each other. The song sparrows and turtledoves are accompanying them.

"Since the weather turned warm, I can hardly wait to see what all comes up out in the flower beds. I see the crocuses and the daffodils. But hyacinths and tulips are coming, too. It's all so new and interesting."

"Did you hear the spring peepers last night?" Joe wondered. "They stir my blood and give me spring fever."

"Hundreds of them. They do make me anxious to get out there. When can we plant the garden? I have my seeds all ready."

"I think it has dried off well enough for disking," Joe replied. "I think I can do it later this forenoon. I can also mix some lime for whitewashing the tree trunks, if you want to do that."

"Oh, no, don't bother," Arie responded. "I never especially liked to see whitewashed trees. I like my trees with a natural look."

"Oh, no! So you're one of Nancy's friends." Joe chuckled. "She'll thank you for that. *Mamm* used to tell us to whitewash the tree trunks until Nancy begged her to leave them as they are. Ya, well, it suits me fine, too."

Arie spent the morning happily cleaning flower beds and putting manure on the raspberry patch. She found clumps of rhubarb and an old asparagus patch. Many old-fashioned flowering perennials were peeking through the damp earth. It was so exciting to see the different plants coming up and to try to identify them.

As for the raspberry patch, it was quite a tangle of brambles. "They're out of control," Arie muttered to herself. "It looks like they haven't been trimmed for ages. I'll get my clippers and trim them before Joe is ready to start planting."

As Arie headed toward the house, she happened to glance across the field and noticed Old Capp and his dog sauntering out his lane to the road. She watched as he disappeared around a the curve.

69

"That's the first time I've seen him go away since we're here," Arie mused aloud. "He has a rattletrap old pickup truck, but I've never seen him use it.

"Hmmm. . . . This would be my chance to do something nice for him, such as giving him a pie. Would I dare? He surely should be pleased with a *Schnitzboi* (dried-apple pie) even though it was made on a Sunday. It wouldn't take me long to run over to his place and back. That's just what I'll do!"

Arie hurried to the house, got the pie out of the gas refrigerator, and wrapped it in plastic wrap. Then she started across the field to the fencerow, where the walking was easier.

What a lovely day! she thought happily. The freshly turned earth, the fragrant breezes that seemed to speak of misty meadowlands and pungent woodlands, and the joyous birds bursting forth in praises to their Creator—it was all so enchanting. Two saucy jays called from a treetop, and a bobwhite whistled from somewhere on the ridge.

"I hope Old Capp likes the birds and the wildlife," Arie murmured. "They sure are abundant back here, and I'm so glad I took the time to do this."

The closer Arie came to Capp's old house, the more appalled she became. It was nothing more than a tumbledown shack. A stack of firewood was piled outside against the house, and a crude bench was on the collapsing porch, beside the open door.

Arie set her pie on the bench. She couldn't resist looking inside, with the door standing wide open like that. A potbellied woodstove was near one wall, with a stovepipe to the ceiling. Stacks of yellowed news-papers were on the floor beside the stove, and behind it was a big pile of tin cans. The floor was so grubby that it looked almost like a dirt floor.

On the shelves along one wall were various old bat-tered pots and pans, tin cups, and pails. Spiderwebs hung from the ceiling above sacks of flour, cornmeal, and rice. In one corner stood a narrow cot, covered by a grimy-looking blanket and an old flat pillow. There was a bucket on a rickety-looking table, and a dipper handle was showing above its rim.

"He must fetch his water from the spring," Arie de-cided. "There's no sign of faucets or running water anywhere. My, how primitive it all is!"

A sudden yell from across the field made Arie whirl around. Her heart beat wildly with fear when she saw Old Capp running in the lane, yelling and waving his arms. His dog had been sniffing out rabbits in the fencerow. Roused to fury, he came running toward Arie as fast as he could, barking and growling fero-ciously.

There was no time to run. Arie stood rooted to the ground, petrified with fear. Why, oh, why, had she lingered to look instead of going straight home? Now she was paying dearly for her curiosity.

"Help, help, Joe!" she called weakly. She looked imploringly to the back field, where Joe was plowing. However, he was far away, headed in the other di-rection with the horses and nearly at the end of the row, not within hearing distance.

The angry dog was getting closer by leaps and

bounds, growling and barking ominously and menacingly. It was like a bad dream, and she was not able to move. Then, without a moment to spare, Arie recovered her wits, grabbed a piece of firewood off the pile, and sprang up on the bench by the door. The dog was there, advancing slowly, growling deep in his throat, his hackles rising and his yellowish eyes gleaming balefully.

Arie raised the piece of wood as if to strike, and the dog growled all the more but came no further. He was poised to charge. Arie shivered but kept a tight grip on the wood, ready to protect herself. Her heart was pounding fiercely.

What if I faint and fall down in front of the dog? Will he tear me to pieces? The suspense was awful. Her lips were moving, praying to God for help.

Then with a yell, Capp came up, puffing and panting. "We've got you trapped now!" he ranted. "What do you mean by coming here thievin' in broad daylight, the minute Wuf and I are out of sight! First you steal my land, and now you want to steal my supplies yet. Aha! We've caught you now." He glared at Arie with fierce hatred in his eyes.

If looks could kill . . . , Arie thought, shuddering. His face was old and leathery, and his unruly white hair gave him a wild look. Some of his teeth were missing; the rest were yellow and tobacco stained.

Arie felt a surge of pity for the old man and decided to try to reason with him. "I didn't come to steal," she said softly. "I wanted to do something nice for you, so I brought you a pie." She pointed to the

Schnitzboi on the bench beside her. "Do you like dried-apple pie?"

The dog had forgotten his anger and was sniffing hungrily at the pie. He grabbed it between his teeth, ran off under a tree with it, tore off the wrapping, and began to gulp it down.

"Hey!" Old Capp yelled shrilly. "She came to poison us, Wuf, that's what she did. Don't eat another bite." He ran over to the dog, grabbed the pie from him, then ran into the house with the half-eaten pie. Wuf, snarling because his food was snatched away, followed at his heels. Capp slammed the door.

For a few moments Arie stood there, wondering if it would be safe to make a dash for home. Finally, summoning all the courage she had, she laid the wood on the bench and began to run. She wanted to carry the wood with her in case Capp let the dog out of the house and sicced him on her. But she would not be accused of stealing even that much.

Arie ran for her life, so it seemed to her, and didn't stop until she collapsed breathless and panting by the raspberry patch in the garden. All was quiet by Capp's house. As she rested, her painful and agonized breathing slowed and quieted. "Whew! That was nearly as bad as being locked in a chest in the attic!" Arie declared, still gasping.

"*Danki Gott* (thank God) that I'm safe at home. I hope when Capp sees that the pie doesn't do his dog any harm, he'll know I meant no harm and was just trying to be neighborly. Poor, poor old man."

She sat there, too exhausted to move, until Joe

came in from the field to disk the garden. *"Ya, well, so geht's wann's gute geht* (yes, well, all's well that ends well)," she murmured as she jumped up to get her garden seeds.

Joe had hitched two horses to the disk and was ready to begin. "I wonder what ails Old Capp," he called to Arie, and motioned toward the old man's place.

Capp sat on the bench outside his door, his head in his hands, the picture of dejection. Beside him sat the dog with his head on Capp's knee.

When Arie told Joe what had happened, he couldn't help scolding her a bit. "Don't ever try it again," he warned. "If you want to give him something, put it in a bag and hang it under his mailbox. Who knows, as angry as Capp is, he might even keep a loaded gun somewhere."

"I'll certainly keep clear of him," Arie promised. "But I sure do pity him. I wonder what thoughts are going through his head right now. Maybe he's realizing all he's missing by holding a grudge for so long and refusing to forgive."

"It could be," Joe agreed. "He's cutting himself off from society and friends. We must remember to pray for him."

Arie forgot her troubles with Capp as she happily dropped the seeds into the furrows and hoed to cover them in rich, dark earth. Robins sang from the cherry tree. Joe cut up the potatoes and planted them while Arie planted peas, red beets, onion sets, parsley, carrots, and lettuce.

She did love garden planting, and this was even more special than usual. It was the first time they had their own garden.

We'll have the garden of of our dreams, Arie thought. With a smile on her lips, she stopped for a moment to gaze back to the chestnut ridge. She was dreaming of the first garden peas, golden ears of corn, and juicy ripe tomatoes.

Plop! Arie was startled out of her reverie as the eye of a potato landed on her apron. Joe was grinning down at her.

"Daydreaming?" he teased.

Arie nodded. "Just taking a few minutes to enjoy the scenery. It's so beautiful."

Joe, however, had eyes only for his young wife. She sat in the garden, her sunbonnet pushed back, dreamily gazing off to the hills. "It's you that makes the beautiful picture," he said, with his heart in his eyes.

Arie felt a surge of joy in her breast at his words. *I can't believe I ever had Heemweh,* she thought. *I won't let things like mice and spiders and even Old Capp spoil my happiness.* Aloud, she said, "Happiness is being your wife and living at Chestnut Ridge Acres!"

10

The Explosion

ON Wednesday at three in the afternoon, Arie noticed that the bread was all. "Oh, dear, what a poor housekeeper I am," she lamented. "What will Joe think? I'd better start bread dough right now so we have some for breakfast."

That day she had been quite busy, working outside. In the morning she found a sizable strawberry patch. Although it was old and neglected, it had a surprising number of nice plants in it. Arie set to work with a will, pulling out all the weeds. When she was finished, she surveyed the patch with a sigh of satisfaction.

"Those plump, juicy berries will taste mighty good in late May and June," she declared. "I'm so glad it's here."

Then there was more cleaning up to do in the house yard and in the *Scheierhof* (barnyard). Thus it was midafternoon when Arie began to think of what she could make for supper. That was when she discovered that there was no more bread.

By then, it was rather late to start bread dough. *Maybe if I put an extra tablespoon of yeast in, it will rise fast enough to be baked before bedtime,* she thought. *Joe will think I'm a poor housekeeper.*

She mixed the dough, kneaded it for twenty minutes, put a clean dishcloth over the bowl, and set it on top of the stove's warming closet to rise.

Taking the stove lifter, she raised the round stove lid to peek inside. "Ach, my," she wailed, "my coal fire went out. We can't do without a fire yet. This stone house will be damp and chilly for at least another month. The bread dough won't rise fast, either, if the kitchen isn't warm. Oh, dear. I'll have to hunt for some kindling and get some kerosene, but I'm busy enough without having to do that yet."

She was extra busy because they, with a van load of others, were planning to go back to their home community early the next morning and spend the day with Arie's parents. So they had to work ahead. They were planning to leave at 4:30 a.m. and probably not get back till ten or eleven at night.

Arie tied a kerchief on her head and hurried to the barn to find kindling. From his stall, Chief greeted her with a whinny, and she paused to give him a few pats on the nose.

Looking around, she sighed, "There's a lot of work

to be done here yet, too. It's not a cheerful place yet."
The front feedway had been cleaned, but in the back
of the barn, huge dust-covered spiderwebs hung from
the ceiling.

Arie found an old wire egg basket and began to
pick up wood chips and old corncobs lying around
on the barn floor. She ducked her head to avoid the
spiderwebs because she didn't want them twined
around her *Kapp* and kerchief. The sound of pigeons
cooing drifted down the hay hole. She knew they
were high up in the barn, resting on beams.

Next she found an old rusty tin can, went to the
kerosene tank beside the barn, and filled it with the
smelly stuff. Holding it at arm's length so it wouldn't
drip on her dress, she carried it and the basket of kindling back to the kitchen.

She stuffed some newspaper into the stove, added
the cobs and wood chips, and poured kerosene over
it all. "Now where did I put the matches?" she sighed.
"Haste makes waste. I must've left them by the lamp
in the *Sitzschtubb* (sitting room)."

Arie was barely out of the kitchen when there was
a terrific explosion behind her. She heard a loud clanging and a fire raging and crackling. For a moment Arie
stood there stunned and unable to move, then she
sprang out the sitting-room door onto the porch.

"Fiah, fiah (fire, fire)!" she yelled at the top of her
lungs. "Joe, Joe, *dapper kumm* (come quickly)!"

Joe had heard the commotion while working in the
implement shed and was already running for the
house at top speed.

"Get the fire extinguisher in the shop!" he shouted to Arie. He yanked open the kitchen door and cautiously entered. The fire was already somewhat subdued, but the flames were still roaring out of the stove. The four round stove lids had been blown off onto the floor. When Joe picked them up with the lifter and put them in place, the roaring stopped.

Arie came running with the extinguisher. "We don't need it after all," Joe said with relief. "Nothing else caught fire There isn't even much smoke damage."

"What—what caused the explosion?" Arie stammered weakly, sinking into a chair.

"I don't know. You didn't pour gas on the fire, did you?" he teased.

"Of course not," Arie retorted. "The fire was out, so I put newspaper and kindling in the stove and poured kerosene over it. When I went to get the matches, it exploded."

Joe reached for Arie and pulled her close. "*Danki Gott* (thank God) you weren't close when it happened," he said with deep feeling. "You could have been badly burned. There must've been some live coals underneath somewhere, and when the kerosene trickled down on them, it exploded.

"After this, pour the kerosene over the cobs and wood outside, before you put them in the stove. And have the match ready to light the fire as soon as you load the stove. But *mei Zeit* (my, my), we sure are *glicklich* (lucky). I guess an angel was watching over you. I know of more than one house that burned down from just such an explosion."

Suddenly Arie was trembling from head to foot, with tears filling her eyes.

"Oh, Joe," she cried. "I don't think I'll ever learn to be a good *Hausfraa* (housewife). I can't even start a fire without nearly burning the house down. We're out of bread, too, and now the dough I started is probably ruined. I feel like a failure. Maybe when we go home tomorrow, I should just stay there."

"Hush," Joe scolded, covering her mouth with his hand. "You talk like a *narrisch Weiber* (foolish woman), like Job told his wife. It wasn't your fault at all! It was mine for not telling you. I knew you weren't used to tending a wood and coal fire and that you had a gas stove at home. I should have taken better care of you. I'm so sorry."

He kissed her tenderly. Arie clung to him for a moment, then thought of her bread dough again. Joe got the bowl down from the warming closet and took off the dishcloth.

"It looks all right to me," he said. "I'll help you clean the kitchen now, and it'll be none the worse for the explosion. Tomorrow we have the day off. It will be great seeing your family again."

The kitchen was soon spick-and-span again, and Arie's discouragement vanished. The bread dough rose beautifully. Just before supper, she was able to put it into the pans. "That should be ready to bake, well before bedtime," she said with a sigh of relief, as she pricked the loaves with a fork.

"Now, what could I make for supper? We can't have sandwiches, for we're out of bread. I guess it'll be potatoes and a can of vegetable soup from the cellar."

By 7:45 the bread dough had risen over the tops of the pans and was ready to bake. Arie lit the old kerosene stove in the washhouse, carried the bread pans out, and carefully slid them in the oven. "That extra yeast sure did the trick," she told herself. "Or maybe it was the explosion. Anyway, it sure rose nice and round."

Joe came in from the barn. "Are you finished with your work?" he asked. "If not, maybe I can help you so we can get to bed early. We have to get up at four to be ready for the van."

"I just want to make some icing and frost the cake I'm taking along," Arie told him. "That shouldn't take more than ten minutes. All you have to do is lick the bowl."

"Sounds good," Joe chuckled, settling down on the easy chair. "I'll read the farm paper till the bowl's ready."

By 8:15 Joe and Arie were ready for bed. Arie set the alarm clock for 4:00, then blew out the kerosene lamp. They knelt together for their *Owedgebet* (evening prayer).

As they climbed into bed, Arie took off her *Kapp* (prayer covering) to put on her *Schlofkapp* (nightcap). After they were settled in bed, she noticed that she had put her *Kapp* in front of the lighted battery alarm clock on the bureau. She could hardly see what time it was through the thin organdy material.

Ach well, I won't get out of bed again, she decided. *If I want to know what time it is, I'll just look closely.*

About two hours later, Arie woke up out of a deep sleep. What had awakened her? She sat up in bed, squinting to see the alarm clock. It was ten o'clock.

"What's wrong," Joe asked, sitting up, too. "Do I smell smoke?"

Joe and Arie jumped out of bed. Smoke? Joe was pulling on his pants. The minute he opened the door to the kitchen, a cloud of burning, scorching air rolled in.

Suddenly it dawned on Arie. "My bread," she gasped. "I forgot to take it out of the oven!"

The washhouse door was open to the kitchen. Arie dashed out to the kerosene stove, her nightgown billowing behind her. She grabbed two pot holders, yanked open the oven door, and clunked the pans with the hard burnt-black remains on the concrete floor.

"How could I have forgotten my bread?" she wailed.

Joe turned off the stove. "What a relief," he said weakly. "For the second time today I thought the house was on fire."

He threw the burned bread, pans and all, out the back washhouse door. "We'll open the windows, and by tomorrow morning the smoke will be gone."

Arie covered her face with her hands and leaned against the kitchen cabinet. *"Des kann net sei* (this just can't be)," she moaned. "This I can't blame on anyone but myself. I sure do feel like a total failure now."

"Nonsense," Joe chided her. "Think of all the good loaves of bread you made since we're here. So don't worry about a few burned ones. You are a good *Hausfraa,* the best wife any man ever had. I couldn't do without you. Come, let's get back to bed."

Joe was soon sleeping again, but Arie tossed and turned. Finally she dozed off, but soon woke again, her heart pounding. She had dreamed that the house was on fire! Soothing, relaxing sleep seemed to be out of the question for her now.

Arie slept fitfully, again and again dozing off, then awaking with a start after a disturbing dream. Finally she fell into a deep sleep, but then it seemed like just a few minutes later when Joe was shaking her.

"Wake up, Arie, it's 4:10," he said in dismay. "The van comes in twenty minutes. Our alarm didn't go off."

Quickly they both jumped out of bed.

"Ach, my, we'll have to hurry," Arie lamented groggily as she groped for a match to light the kerosene lamp. "It seems like I hardly slept at all."

"I'll quickly feed the horses and milk the cow while you make some breakfast," Joe said, jumping into his pants. "At least we have twenty minutes."

Arie dressed, built up the fire in the cookstove, and put the black iron frying pan on it. She added butter, then thick slices of mush. As soon as that was browned, she would fry the eggs.

Quickly she closed all the windows. The odor of the burned bread still hung heavy, but it wouldn't be right to leave with all the windows wide open. There would be no time to take a bath, as she had planned to do.

Arie took off her *Schlofkapp* and quickly combed her wavy hair into submission, pulled it tightly back into place, and made her hair bob. She went into the bedroom for her *Kapp*. When she picked it up, she gasped. The alarm clock said 11:30! She stared at it and could not believe what she saw.

Joe came in from the barn. "You won't need to fry any mush for me," he called to Arie as he washed his hands at the wash bowl. "I'm just not hungry yet."

"Come and look at this alarm clock," Arie said in astonishment. "You won't believe it. *Es is ken Wunner* (it's no wonder) that we're not hungry yet."

Joe stared at the clock, then whistled in amazement. *"Was in die Welt* (what in the world)!" he exclaimed. "How could I have been so wrong?"

Arie began to laugh. "I love the expression on your face," she giggled. "Now we have five hours to get ready, thanks to you."

"Ei yi yi," Joe said sheepishly. "I sure disturbed our sleep. No wonder the horses seemed to be too sleepy to eat, and the cow didn't have much milk. Ya, well, now you know you're not the only one around here who makes mistakes. Let's get back to bed."

Snuggled under the covers, Arie smothered another giggle. Maybe sometime she would tell Joe that her *Kapp* was in front of the alarm clock. That was likely why he had misread it. But for now, she was just so tickled that *she* hadn't been the one who roused them before it was time.

She hung her daytime *Kapp* on the bedpost this time and put on her *Schlofkapp* again. *I've made enough mistakes for a while,* she decided, smiling in the darkness. *It was Joe's turn, and it makes me feel better.*

"So geht's," she murmured sleepily. "All's well that ends well."

11

Nancy at Chestnut Ridge Acres

THE house was stirring with excitement as Nancy hurriedly washed the breakfast dishes. Today was the day the whole family was planning to travel by van to visit Joe and Arie at Chestnut Ridge Acres. They had not seen Joe and Arie for six weeks, not since the young couple had come home for a one-day visit in the early spring.

School had let out two weeks ago, and Steven had packed his clothes to stay for the rest of the summer at the Chestnut Ridge Farm and work for his brother. Nancy was going to stay, too, until the dairy barn raising! She could hardly believe her good fortune.

That might be two weeks or more, depending on how long it took to get ready. There was a lot of work to be done before the frolic.

"I just hope I won't have to sleep in the dog room," Nancy said to *Mamm* (Mom), who was combing the little girls' hair. "I don't think I could stand it after what Joe said it looked like."

Just then Steven came in with the milk and heard what Nancy said. "Don't you worry! You won't get the chance," he declared. "I want that room, if Arie doesn't mind. It has the best view over the chestnut ridge, and I might be able to see deer and bear early in the morning. I don't care how many dogs used to live there."

"Dummel dich (hurry up) and get ready, Steven," Mamm interrupted. "I'm afraid the van will be here before we're ready. Is Omar in from the barn already? Nancy, pack those shoofly pies and jars of jam into a big box. Wrap the jars in newspaper so they won't break. And don't forget the two containers of cup cheese in the refrigerator."

"I can't find my shoes," Henry called down the stairs.

"Go barefooted then," Steven shot back. "I guess you didn't put them where they belong."

They were hustling and bustling to be ready in time. Ten minutes later the van drove in the lane.

"Here we go, ready or not," *Daed* (Dad) announced. "Omar, you can carry the big box."

"Get your bonnets, girls," Mamm instructed. "There are some last-minute things to do yet, but we'll just leave them."

87

Outside it was still dark, and the stars were shining. Nancy climbed into the van and headed for the backseat, glad to have the chance to sit by the window. *I won't mind the bouncing if the driver turns on his music,* she thought. *Back here I'll be able to hear it better anyway.*

"*Ich bin so froh* (I'm so glad)," little Lydia said, squirming with excitement. "I can't wait to see Joe and Arie again."

"Mary and Jacob will be there, too, and little Nancy Ann," Mamm told her.

"Ooooh, I want to hold her first," Susie squealed. "Are we about there?"

"No, it'll take a while yet. And you will have to take turns holding the baby," Mamm instructed. "Be sure you don't fight over who gets to hold her first."

The sun soon rose in the east as the van headed northwest, toward the Summerville settlement.

"Two whole weeks at Joe's!" Nancy exulted. "What if my 'little visit' there lasts as long as it did at Mary and Jacob's? I sure wish I could get to see Sally and Andrew again, somehow or other. If only they would live closer to Joe's place."

The three hours of driving seemed long. Everyone was glad when at last they crossed the narrow bridge and they could see Chestnut Ridge Acres.

"Look at the ridge!" Steven exclaimed. "It's green. I can't wait to go back there and see the wildlife."

"There's Joe," Nancy squealed, "standing by the barn, waiting for us. And, look, he has a beard. I forgot that he has a beard now."

Everyone laughed. The driver stopped the van and rolled down the window. "That's a fine beard you have there," he teased good-naturedly. "What did you do, put fertilizer on it?"

Joe grinned. "Nope, just watered it," he bantered back. "Did you forget to water yours?"

Lydia was out of the van in a flash. "Joe! Joe!" she cried, running to him. He caught her and swung her up in the air. Suddenly he realized how much he had missed his family. It was so good to see them all again.

Arie came out of the house to welcome them. "Do come in," she invited. "We're so glad to see you all."

"There come Jacob and Mary," Henry announced. "That's King hitched to the *Dachwegli* (carriage)."

The girls ran off to meet them and to hold Nancy Ann. It was a happy family reunion, a time for visiting as well as working. The menfolk got busy drawing up plans for the new dairy barn and consulting with *Zimmer* (head-carpenter) Mose. They ordered the needed lumber and supplies.

Mamm had brought along a wall hanging to put into the frame. The womenfolk would quilt it while visiting. This would give them something to do besides cooking for the men. When it was finished, she would sell the wall hanging to a lady in town.

Arie already had the potatoes peeled and the beef roasting in the range. The women had time to take a stroll outside and survey Arie's garden.

"It looks like you'll soon have a lot of strawberries to pick," Mamm observed. "They're nice and big already. You sure can use Nancy's help for that."

"Yes, I'm so glad she can stay," Arie agreed. "I think I'll have a lot more than I need for our own use. We'll probably take the extras to the grocery store in town. That'll give me some pin money."

Mamm and Mary admired Arie's neat garden. Rows of blooming sugar peas would soon be ready to pick. The peas, heads of lettuce and cabbage, tiny sweet corn, and newly set-out tomato plants looked so fresh and tidy.

Out in a side patch, she had planted watermelons and cantaloupes and rows and rows of potatoes.

"My, I can't believe how much better your yard and the entire place look since the last time I saw it," Mamm exclaimed. "You sure must've worked! Your flower beds are as pretty as a picture, too."

"It was hard work," Arie admitted. "I'm glad for all I got done. In the next few weeks, we're going to be busier than ever."

"Look!" Susie cried. "There goes that old man and his dog."

Old Capp was walking out the fencerow toward the chestnut ridge.

"Be sure to stay away from his place," Arie warned. She told about her frightening experience when she took a *Schnitzboi* (dried-apple pie) to Capp.

"I'm trying to think of what we could do for him to try to soften his heart, besides giving him food. He would just think we were trying to poison him."

As they stood watching him, Capp turned, brandished his walking stick threateningly at them, then sauntered out the field lane.

"See," Arie sighed, "he's that mad at us. All because of a boundary-line dispute years ago."

"The poor man," Mamm sympathized. "If only he could realize the harm he's doing to himself by his unforgiving spirit. Maybe there are other things he's bitter about, too. About the only thing you can do is to try to return good for evil and pray for him."

Mamm looked around the room. "Ya, well, let's get that wall hanging into the frame."

"Where will we set it up?" Arie wondered. "My kitchen is too small."

"Why not upstairs in the dog room?" Mary teased. "But then Nancy might not help quilt."

"That's right, I wouldn't," Nancy declared, not caring if they laughed at her. "I'll hold Nancy Ann instead while I have the chance. I'm not fond of quilting anyway."

"Ach, I know just the place," Arie decided, "the small room above the *Kammer* (downstairs bedroom). It's completely empty except for a bench we store up there. From there we'll have a view to the barn so we can see what the men are doing."

Soon the small quilt frame was set up and the wall hanging pinned into place, first the backing, then the fluffy Dacron, and last the appliquéd top.

"It's beautiful," Mary admired it. "I'd like to have a big quilt like this for a bed."

"May we go up and explore the attic?" Susie asked. She was thinking it might be full of interesting old stuff like the attic at home—maybe even some old dolls or doll furniture.

Arie laughed. "You may go up, but you'll be disappointed. There's not much there but a few empty boxes."

Undaunted, the two little girls trudged up the attic stairs. Suddenly the quilters heard a muffled cry, then a cracking sound. Two feet emerged from the ceiling.

"Help, help," Susie cried in a panic-stricken voice. The next thing she knew she was hanging by her arms from an old stovepipe hole in the ceiling and near an inside wall.

"*Unvergleichlich* (weird)!" Mamm exclaimed. "Grab her quick, before she falls!"

Nancy stood up on a chair to get Susie. "Oh, dear, she's stuck," Nancy cried. "What shall we do?"

Arie and Mary rushed up the attic stairs and in a moment had pulled Susie to safety. Her outstretched arms had prevented her from falling through.

As soon as Susie realized she wasn't hurt, she began to laugh, and the others laughed with her.

"It looks liked you started to come down faster than you went up," Arie chuckled. "I see that there was just an old piece of insulation over the stovepipe hole. I'll have to get Joe to nail a board over it."

The rest of the day passed quickly and happily. The girls took turns holding and playing with Nancy Ann while the women were preparing the meal, quilting, and visiting. Soon it was time for the family to start for home—all but Steven and Nancy, who were staying.

Plans had been made for the barn raising in two weeks. *Zimmer* Mose had scheduled workers to prepare necessary things in advance: the footer, the foundation, the barn floor, and the timbered framework. Then on barn-raising day, the sections of framework would be set up in place for the dairy barn. A swarm of men would put on the siding and the roof.

When the van drove in the lane and the rest of the Petersheim family got in, Nancy felt the familiar funny feeling inside, a feeling almost like *Heemweh* (homesickness), but it passed quickly. She really did look forward to her stay at Joe and Arie's place. Besides, Steven was there to keep her company.

"Good-bye, good-bye," Susie and Lydia called in unison.

"*Schaffet hatt* (work hard)," Henry called out the window.

"*Mir waerre* (we will)," Steven answered.

Nancy and Steven stood watching as the van wound its way out the lane, over the narrow bridge, and out of sight. Old Capp and his dog were watching, too, from the window of his old house, and he shook his fist at them.

12

Thumps in the Night

WHEN bedtime came, Steven got his wish to have the dog room. Nancy was assigned to the bedroom next to the quilting room. Mamm had decided to leave the wall hanging in the frame. The Summerville women could work on it when they came with their husbands to help get ready for the frolic.

Joe couldn't resist teasing Nancy and Steven a bit. "If you hear screams in the night, don't be frightened. It's just our panther up on the chestnut ridge, or maybe a screech owl."

Steven's eyes widened. "I sure wish there were a panther back there, or even just a bobcat. Did you really ever hear screams?"

"Not yet," Joe chuckled. "But we did see bear tracks."

Nancy repressed a shiver. She had memories of being afraid she would meet a bear when she was a little girl. And here there was actually a possibility!

"Don't let him scare you," Arie comforted. "We never saw a bear, and I don't think any would come near the buildings."

Arie led the way to Nancy's room and lit the kerosene lamp. "There's an extra blanket in the chest if you get cool," she said. "Or you can take the screen out of one of the windows and close it."

When Arie left, Nancy sat on the chest, gazing out the screened window into the darkness. A warm breeze swayed the curtains gently. She heard frogs croaking somewhere far off. A dog barked sharply, then was silent.

"Old Capp's dog," Nancy muttered. "What if he and his dog are out prowling around tonight?" She wished her room didn't face Capp's place. But the night seemed friendly enough, with the night insects singing and the moon shining through the trees.

"Nancy."

Nancy jumped, startled at the whisper in the darkness. Steven stood in the doorway of her room.

"Don't scare me like that," she scolded. "What are you sneaking around for?"

"Let's walk back to the chestnut ridge," Steven urged. He spoke in a soft voice to keep from waking Joe and Arie. "I've got my twelve-volt spotlight. I'm sure we could spot a lot of wildlife. Deer, and bears, and bobcats . . ."

"Are you serious?" Nancy exclaimed. "For all you

know, Old Capp's prowling around back there, ready to sic his dog on us. Maybe he even carries a gun, as bitter as he is."

"I'm not scared of Capp and his dog," Steven protested. "He's just a harmless old man, and I plan to make friends with his dog as soon as I can."

"Ya, well, we won't go without Joe's permission," Nancy declared. "Maybe he and Arie will go with us sometime."

"Ah, c'mon, you're just chicken," Steven pouted. "Joe's not our dad. Besides, he's in bed already. I think you're just scared. I guess I'll go alone, then."

"Please don't," Nancy implored. "I promise to go with you sometime if we have Joe's permission."

"All right then." Steven finally gave it up. "We'll see if you keep your word." He left for the dog room.

I hope he knows I meant in the daytime, not at night, Nancy thought as she closed the door. She quickly undressed, donned her nightgown, and knelt to say her bedtime prayers. Then she sank into the soft bed.

The door to the room with the wall hanging stood open. Nancy chuckled as she remembered how Susie had looked, dangling from the stovepipe hole. As she was drifting off to sleep, she again heard Old Capp's dog barking, and she snuggled under the sheet. "I'm glad I'm not out there," she murmured happily. Then she drifted off to dreamland.

How long she slept, she did not know, but suddenly she was wide awake, her heart pounding. *Thump, thump, thump!* What was that? It seemed to be right there in her room. In her half-awake confusion, she imagined it was Capp's dog under her bed. Cold fear gnawed at her.

There it was again. *Thump, thump, thump!* Nancy ducked under the sheet, her heart racing wildly. Was it a dog, or had the panther jumped through her window? *Thump, thump, thump!* It sounded like a bear walking.

The room was pitch dark. Nancy could stand it no longer. "Steven, help!" she called loudly. The sound of her own voice in the stillness of the night frightened her even more. There it was again: *Thump, thump, thump!*

"Steven!" she yelled, at the top of her lungs.

Joe came running out of the *Kammer* (downstairs bedroom) and up the steps, two at a time. He nearly collided with Steven, who was racing down the hall with his spotlight in hand and his eyes huge.

"What's wrong?" Steven called.

"Is the house on fire?" Joe asked right away.

"There's something in my room," Nancy cried. "Shine your flashlight all around."

Joe grabbed the light from Steven and directed its beam into the corners. "I don't see anything."

There it was again: *Thump, thump, thump!* He shone the light toward the sound. In the doorway to the next room, there was an ugly-looking bat, blinking its beady eyes.

Arie came running up the stairs, too, wearing an apron over her nightgown.

"It's just a bat," Joe said. "Steven, go get a broom."

He struck a match and lit the kerosene lamp.

"I know where it came from," Arie exclaimed. She pointed to the stovepipe hole above the wall hanging. "That's where Susie fell through, and we didn't get around to covering the hole again."

"Bats in the attic," Joe muttered.

Steven came running with the broom. Nancy ducked under the sheets while Joe advanced on the bat. After a few whacks, he announced triumphantly, "There, *es is dot* (it's dead)!"

"Are you sure it's the only one that came down?" Nancy asked, peeking out from under the covers.

"We'll search the rooms thoroughly," Joe promised. "But first we'll cover the hole in the attic."

That done, he shone the spotlight into every nook and cranny until they were certain that there was no other bat in Nancy's room or in the other rooms upstairs.

"Do you want to sleep downstairs on the sitting-room sofa for the rest of the night?" Arie asked Nancy. "I wouldn't blame you if you wouldn't want to sleep in this room anymore."

"Oh, no, I'll be all right," Nancy reassured her. "As soon as I knew what it was, I wasn't scared anymore."

"Just be glad it didn't try to build a nest in your hair," Steven teased.

After everyone had gone back to bed and Nancy had blown out the lamp, she lay awake for a long time. When she finally did doze off, a few minutes later she awoke again, her heart pounding. Had she heard a scream from the direction of the chestnut ridge, or had she just imagined it?

Old Capp's dog was barking again, so he must've heard something too. She lay quietly, straining to hear it again, but all was quiet.

"Ya, well, I guess it was just a dream," she told herself. "The dog was probably barking at the moon."

13

A Barrel of Wood

"SUMMER seems to have come in a hurry," Joe remarked at the dinner table. "It's not often that we have such a warm spell this early. It feels like it could reach ninety in the shade. Steven and I will have to *schaufle* (cultivate) the garden patch this afternoon with one of the workhorses."

"The heat is ripening the strawberries fast, too," Arie said happily. "I'm so glad they're early so Nancy can help me pick them while she's here. We picked twenty-five quart boxes this forenoon. That makes us extra busy since we're preparing food for the workers, too."

"What will you do with them? Can them?" Steven asked.

"Oh, no, not the first ones," Arie told him. "They're so nice and big, and we get a high price for them.

"Joe, could we have Chief this afternoon, to take them to Mrs. Shprecher at the grocery store in town? We need some stuff anyway. Since Nancy is here to go with me, you won't need to take time off from your work."

"Sure, I'll hitch him to the market wagon right after dinner," Joe promised. "Better get plenty of supplies. We'll be sure to have workers to feed nearly every day for a while. Next week we'll be even busier than this week, what with getting ready for the frolic."

As soon as the dishes were washed, Arie and Nancy put the boxes of berries in cardboard boxes and loaded them into the market wagon. True to his word, Joe had hitched Chief to the wagon and tied him by the barn door.

Joe and Steven were already busy in the garden patch. Steven was riding the workhorse, and Joe was guiding the *Schaufleleeg* (cultivator) that was hitched to the horse. Up and down the rows they went, *schaufling* out the weeds.

"Won't Mrs. Shprecher be pleased with these nice berries?" Arie remarked. "She said she'll take all I have. And the berries couldn't be nicer."

"Look!" Nancy said, pointing toward Old Capp's place. "There he is again, sitting on the bench beside his door, with his head bent low. Do you think he's that sad?"

"I think so. I know I would be if I held such a grudge against someone. For each minute of anger, I

101

would lose sixty seconds of happiness," Arie replied.

"Hey, why don't we stop at his mailbox and leave a box of strawberries there for him?" Arie proposed. "Somehow, I don't believe he really thinks I tried to poison him with that pie."

Then she called out, "Whoa, Chief." The horse stopped by Capp's mailbox. "Nancy, put a box of berries in this plastic grocery bag. Here's a piece of twine to tie it under the mailbox."

Arie took a scrap of paper out of her handbag and wrote on it, "For Capp. Have a nice day. From the Petersheims." Arie handed the note to Nancy to put with the berries.

"There, that ought to make him happy. I hope he enjoys them."

"I'd like to see his face when he finds them." Nancy chuckled as she climbed back in. "I sure hope he doesn't stomp them into the dirt."

Arie let Chief walk most of the way to town, for the sun beat down without mercy. Even so, a white lather of sweat appeared on his legs. "I'm glad we don't have to go far in this heat," Arie commented. "We'll have to hose him down when we get back, to cool him off."

As they turned into the parking lot of Mrs. Shprecher's grocery store, Arie exclaimed, *"Well, guck mol datt* (just look at that). They put up a railing for us to hitch Chief."

"Isn't that nice!" Nancy agreed. She hopped out to tie the horse securely.

Mrs. Shprecher herself came out to greet them.

Although she was *Englisch* (non-Amish), she wore a plain-looking dress. She was plump and kindly looking, and her hair, streaked with gray, was pulled back into a bun.

She looks just as if she ought to be wearing a Kapp (prayer covering) yet, Nancy thought.

"Aren't you pleased?" she asked. "I put that tie railing there for your horse." Then she noticed the berries. "Oh, my goodness, berries already," she exclaimed. "And such nice ones, too. I can't believe it! My customers will certainly be happy."

She pulled two large carrots and an apple out of a bag. "Here's a treat for your horse for bringing the berries." She beamed. "I used to ride horseback when I was a child, and I still love horses. Sixty years ago my dad used to farm with horses."

She patted Chief on the neck and smoothed his mane. "Can he eat this stuff with a bit in his mouth?" she asked.

"Oh, yes," Arie assured her. "Just watch that he doesn't happen to bite your hand."

Mrs. Shprecher fed Chief the carrots piece by piece, stroking his mane as she did so.

"We appreciate it that you had this tie railing put up," Arie said. "I'm sure you'll get more Amish customers now."

"That's the idea," Mrs. Shprecher responded.

Inside the store, she paid them generously for the berries, and Arie even had money left over after buying her groceries.

"We'll have some more berries for you on Thursday,"

Arie told her. "Likely twice as many as today. Could you possibly drive out to pick them up? They should be ready by ten o'clock."

"Okay, I'll come out there," Mrs. Shprecher promised. "Save your horse some trips in this heat. It sure is early for such a heat wave, isn't it? But it won't last long. The latest risk-free date for frost isn't past yet. Next week we could be shivering again and trying to keep our tomato plants from freezing." She chuckled at the idea.

Arie and Nancy said good-bye and carried their grocery bags out to their rig.

"My, isn't she friendly and talkative!" Nancy remarked, as Arie untied Chief and backed him away from the railing.

Arie nodded. "She seems real common and *demiedich* (humble), too. It just seems like she ought to be wearing a *Kapp* yet."

Nancy smiled. "That's just what I was thinking. Why do you think she doesn't?"

"I suppose it's not what she's been taught. I guess she interprets that part of the Bible differently from what we do, where it says that women ought to wear a prayer covering.

"You know, if a woman is selfish and headstrong, wearing a prayer covering doesn't mean a thing. We can be thankful that we live in a country where we have freedom of religion and can do what we feel is right."

When they drove into the barnyard at Chestnut Ridge Acres, Steven came to put away the horse for them. He was chuckling to himself. "You should have seen what I saw awhile ago! I think old Capp stole some strawberries from you somehow. Anyway, I saw him walking along beside the fencerow carrying a box of them and eating berries as fast as he could. He was probably feeling sneaky and guilty."

"No, he didn't steal them," Arie explained. "We hung those berries under his mailbox. I'm glad to hear that he was eating them. That means he trusts us a little more and has quit thinking we're trying to poison him. Maybe sometime he'll be a friend instead of an enemy."

That evening when they were at the supper table, there was a tap, tap, tap on the door. Nancy got up to peek out the window. She gasped, "It's Old Capp and his dog!"

Joe quickly went to the door. "Hello," he said, not knowing what to expect.

"Howdy." Capp spoke in a cackling voice, revealing a yellowed set of teeth, with several of them missing. "I came to git some more of them strawberries. I kin split some wood to pay for 'em."

"Wait a minute."

Joe went back to the table to consult with Arie. "He wants to split some wood for us in exchange for berries. We don't need any more wood this spring, do we?"

"Let's just give him the berries," Arie suggested. "He must be fond of them."

"But I'm afraid that might insult him." Joe pondered the matter for a few seconds. "Maybe he doesn't want to take charity."

"Ya, well, I suppose we might need some kindling

yet. Summer's not here to stay, and it will surely give some cool mornings and evenings yet, when we will start a bit of wood fire. Let him chop all the kindling he wants."

Joe went out to the woodpile with Capp, and his dog trailed along behind them. Steven quickly grabbed a few chicken scraps from the table and hurried outside. Here was his chance. The dog was sniffing out a rabbit trail, with his nose to the ground.

"Here, pup," he said softly. He hoped Old Capp was hard of hearing. Cautiously he threw a chicken scrap to the dog and was rewarded when the eager dog pounced on it and gobbled it up. Then the dog came close to Steven, his tail wagging and his eyes asking for more.

Steven threw another scrap, and the dog even let Steven caress his ears after the food was gone. "You poor beast," Steven murmured. "You're not a vicious cur at all, just a hungry dog so thin that your ribs show. You shall have some beef scraps and a beef bone, too."

Joe handed the ax to Capp and brought an old barrel from the shed. "We could use some kindling, rather than big pieces of wood. Be careful that you don't chop your foot."

"I want four boxes of strawberries," Capp demanded gruffly. "You put them under that there tree, and I'll get them."

He retreated to the other side of the woodpile with the ax. "C'mon, Wuf," he called to his dog. "You stay right here."

Arie and Nancy were watching from the window. "You can pick four boxes of berries," Joe told them through the screen. "Put them under the maple tree, and he'll find them there."

"All right," Arie answered. "I'm thinking that what I suspected is true. He's probably pitifully poor, with hardly enough money for him and his dog to live on. They're both thin and probably half starved. We'll give him more than he asked for, heaped up and running over for good measure."

"You have a heart of gold," Joe told her.

He smiled as he walked to the barn. "Ya, Arie is a jewel of a wife," he murmured, "and I hope I'm worthy of her."

As soon as the berries were put under the tree in a cardboard box, and Arie and Nancy were inside, Capp went for them. He and his dog headed across the field for home.

"He's eating them already," Nancy chuckled, watching from the window. "It evens looks like the dog is eating the stems."

"Let's go out and see the wood that he chopped," Arie said. "I didn't hear much chopping going on. Maybe he only pretended to work."

Joe stood at the barn doorway. "Just look at that," he exclaimed. "Capp sure must be *hattschaffich* (hardworking). It looks like he filled up the barrel and heaped it high. He must be one fast worker. Ei, yi, yi, I can't believe it."

Steven came around the corner of the barn. "Pooh!" he scoffed. "*Hattschaffich* indeed. I watched him, the lazy bum. Just go look at the wood he chopped."

Curiously, the others walked to the woodpile. The barrel was upside down, with a round log on top and bits of kindling heaped around and over the log! The kindling he had actually split was just a small amount.

Joe burst out laughing when he saw it, and Arie and Nancy joined in. "He may be lazy, but he sure is clever," Arie said. "I never would've thought of that."

"It is true," Joe admitted, "that I didn't say how much wood he had to chop. I guess he thought we wouldn't let him have the berries if it wasn't a lot."

Yet Arie was disappointed. Her hopes that Capp would become their friend were fading. Was something good hiding under the vicious front Capp put on? If the Petersheims were friendly, would that bring out something fine?

I guess it's not just a front. He seems to be bitter to the core, she thought sadly. *There's not much hope that he'll ever change.*

14

An Evening Prowler

ARIE had been right. The next picking of berries yielded over forty quarts. By the end of the week, they picked over sixty quarts in one day. She stashed the earnings in a little wooden cheese box.

"My cash box is filling up fast," Arie told Joe on Saturday evening. They were sitting on the porch, watching the dusk descend over the countryside. A soft breeze carried the delightful scent of freshly cut hay and the sweet fragrance of the wild rose bushes below the garden.

"The strawberry money is yours to use however you wish," Joe promised. "Buy yourself something you've always wanted."

"I have my laying hens now," Arie said with a sigh

of satisfaction. "When I have to eat those white eggs from the grocery store with the pale, watery yolks, it just about takes away my appetite for eggs. Besides, they're much too expensive. Give me freshly laid brown eggs any day. I wouldn't mind having a pure-bred pup, though, sometime. I'm used to having a dog on the place."

"So am I," Joe agreed. "What breed would you like?"

"I'm not sure, but I think I'd like a small dog, one that's housebroken for indoors."

"That's fine with me," Joe chuckled. "You're quite different from my mom. She never let us bring any of our dogs into the house. Mamm sure put her foot down about that."

Arie smiled as she imagined her mother-in-law standing at the door with her hands on her hips, scolding, while little Joe, with his arms around his puppy and his eyes pleading, begged to come in.

Aloud, she said, "Ach, ya, but that was different. I wouldn't want big farm dogs in the house either. They're always dragging home dead things and half-eaten game. I think it would be nice to have a farm dog for outdoors and a small house dog, too. Maybe we could raise pups to sell."

"I'll talk to Jacob about it," Joe decided. "Didn't he say their collie's having a litter this summer? And we'll have to ask around to learn where we could get a small dog to suit you, maybe a Pomeranian."

"I know they're expensive," Arie said. "But if I'd get a female and sell the puppies . . . And next week I should be making at least as much with the berries as I did this week."

"Hush," Joe said, tweaking her chin and pulling her close. "You're a *gute Fraa* (good wife), and you shall have whatever you want."

Steven and Nancy had gone for a walk back to the chestnut ridge after supper, even though it was still unseasonably warm. Steven carried Joe's double-barreled twelve-gauge shotgun, in case he saw some thievin' crows or starlings.

Thunderheads piled up in the west, and heat lightning flashed now and then on the horizon, bringing some hope that the weather would turn cooler after a rain. They trudged up the slope, panting from heat and exertion.

"Why did you bring a gun?" Nancy said accusingly. "I want to hear the birds singing and feel the peace and beauty of the evening. If you shoot, you'll shatter it all and scare away all the wildlife. It's so beautiful back here."

"Well, okay, I won't shoot if you don't want me to," Steven agreed. "I don't want to scare off the deer." Deep down he knew that carrying the gun was mostly an ego booster. He didn't really expect to do any hunting tonight.

Reaching the top, Nancy suddenly stopped in her tracks. "Shhh!" she whispered, hardly daring to breathe. "*Guck mol datt* (look there once)."

Barely five hundred feet ahead stood a graceful white-tailed doe with a fawn at her side.

Steven drew in his breath sharply, and his fingers automatically tightened their grip on the gun. For a moment the deer stood there motionless. Then with great bounds, they leaped over logs and brush and disappeared into the woods.

Nancy lifted the binoculars hanging from a strap around her neck. The woods were still alive with birdsong, each feathered package nearly bursting with praise to its Creator. There was a flash of vivid color from a bush. A scarlet tanager! It sat quietly for a moment, then flew away.

Steven and Arie walked on, not talking now. There was too much to see. Near a rocky outcropping, they were startled by a shrill whistle. They saw a groundhog disappearing into its den. A flash of blue in the trees prompted Nancy to lift her binoculars again, and she was rewarded by seeing an indigo bunting flit from branch to branch.

All these beauties of nature and the occasional flashes of heat lightning gave her a feeling of smallness before a great God, the Creator of all these beauties.

They walked the length of the ridge and back, enjoying the beauties of springtime and the marvelous scenery.

Then Nancy reluctantly said, "Ya, well, we'd better get home now, before the bears are out. "

She meant it half teasingly, but it was getting rather dark and— Suddenly they heard several shrill screams from the other side of the ridge.

Nancy grabbed Steven's arm. "Is it a panther?" she asked fearfully, shivering in spite of the heat.

Steven laughed aloud. "Coons," he said scornfully. "They're fighting. I think they're plentiful back here or they wouldn't already be scrapping this early in the evening. We'd better watch the sweet corn in the patch or the coons will get it all."

Nancy sighed with relief. *Just coons!* But she was eager to get home now. Being on the ridge in the dark was not for her. "There's Joe and Arie on the porch," she told Steven when they were close to the house. "Let's go and join them."

In a few minutes they sank down on the porch steps, grateful for the rest and a chance to cool off.

"Boy, it's *wunderbaar schee* (marvelously beautiful) back there," Steven exclaimed. "I wish I'd have a tent and could spend some nights sleeping out on the ridge. I can hardly wait till the hunting and trapping season opens. I'll make sure I'm here then."

"It's just delightful," Arie said, "even when the weather's too warm for comfort. I'd like to see it in the early morning sometime, when the dew is over everything and all is fresh and bright. I believe it would be indescribably awesome." She fanned herself with the farm paper lying on the porch.

Another flash of heat lightning zipped from cloud to cloud, and a cool breeze sprang up. "My, that's refreshing," Arie said gratefully. "I'm hoping we'll have a real thundershower that will clear the air and end the heat wave."

She went inside to the refrigerator and brought out a pitcher of lemonade. "It's hard to believe now, but according to Mrs. Shprecher, they're predicting much cooler weather next week. Maybe we'll even have to watch out for frost yet. I know the weather sure can change fast in the spring."

Joe emptied his glass of lemonade, then got up and stretched. "Time for bed, if we want to get up early for church tomorrow. Steven, be sure to unload that gun and put it back in the cabinet where it belongs."

"Do you mind if I keep the gun in my room?" Steven coaxed. "Yesterday morning a bunch of crows were raising a ruckus in the walnut tree, and I sure did wish I had a gun handy. I think they're doing some crop damage in the field back close to the ridge. I noticed that something's been scratching the planted corn kernels out of the ground. It's either the crows or the blackbirds."

"It could be pheasants, too," Joe said. "But okay, just as long as you're careful. If you never keep the gun loaded, I guess it won't hurt. Since the fields are so close to the ridge, I'm afraid we can expect a lot more crop damage before the year is over. The deer seem to be plentiful, too."

"Say," Steven said excitedly, a thought just popping into his head, "if a farmer has crop damage, he's allowed to hunt the culprits anytime, even though the season for them is otherwise closed. That means I could hunt all summer. Hurrah!"

"Whoa, not so fast here," Joe cautioned. "Don't go shooting anything without my consent. I think we'd have to get permission from the game commission, anyway. We don't want to get in trouble with the game warden."

"Shucks," Steven muttered, as he trudged up the stairs to his room. "I wish Joe wouldn't be such a spoilsport."

He went to the open window in his room, breathing in the cool night air.

A flash of lightning zipped from cloud to earth, and a rumble of far-off thunder followed. *Maybe we will get a storm yet,* he thought hopefully. He moved to the other window. In the next flash of lightning, Steven thought he saw a movement in the field below, not far from the barn.

He watched closely, waiting for the next flash. There! His heartbeat quickened. It was Old Capp and his dog, slowly moving along the fencerow, then over the lane and toward the barn. Each flash of lightning revealed his progress. Steven shrank back, peeping from behind the curtain, watching to see what Capp would do next.

For a full ten minutes, Capp did not move. The dog was at his side. Then he turned slowly and followed the fencerow back to his cabin.

"Hmmm, I wonder what he was up to," Steven muttered. "Was he planning to steal something and didn't quite have the courage? Or was he just out for a stroll?"

Steven climbed into bed and pulled the sheet over himself. The air coming in the window definitely was much cooler. For a while a storm seemed to be moving in. It began to rain, but then it gradually faded away, moving off to the south as Steven drifted off into slumberland.

15

Chicken Thieves

CLOSE to midnight, Steven was suddenly awakened. He sat up in bed, his sleepy brain trying to grasp what the ruckus was all about. Then it dawned on him. Arie's chickens! They were squawking and cackling as if someone were trying to catch them.

Steven was wide awake, and he sprang out of bed and into his trousers. "That's Old Capp for sure," he growled. "Stealing chickens. Now I know what he had in mind when he stood there by the barn. He probably saw us move those chickens up there on the second floor of the barn and knew just where they were."

A plan was forming in Steven's mind. By the light of his flashlight, he struck a match and lit the kerosene lamp. "I'll show that old man a thing or two," he muttered.

Trembling with excitement, he grabbed the gun from the corner. The shells were on the dresser where he had placed them last night. He slipped two shells into the gun and quickly took the screen out of the window. Thankfully, the window stayed up by itself.

Steven's hands shook as he cocked both hammers and braced himself. Then, pointing the gun to the sky, he pulled the triggers. Bang! Bang! The roar of the gun shattered the peace of the surrounding countryside and echoed across the silent hills and valleys.

"If that doesn't scare the dickens out of that old man, I don't know what will," Steven gloated, his ears ringing from the noise.

He peered out into the night, wishing for more lightning. He hoped to see Capp and his dog hightailing it for home, but he was disappointed. There was no moon in sight, and the farm was deeply dark. The chickens had quieted down. All was calm outside now.

Nancy came out of her room, white and trembling. "Steven, *was is letz* (what's wrong)?" she asked, looking fearful and bewildered.

Joe came up the steps at top speed, and Arie was not far behind. "Did the gun go off?" Joe asked quickly, with an unbelieving look on his face.

Steven grinned, sheepishly. "Yes, it did, but not accidentally. Didn't you hear the ruckus the hens were making? I'm sure it was Capp, trying to steal them."

Somehow, with Joe's shocked and disapproving

eyes boring into him, it didn't seem like such a good idea anymore. "I just shot up into the sky," Steven said lamely, his eyes downcast.

He hastened to explain how he had seen Capp and his dog standing by the barn after Joe and Arie were in bed. "So I just shot up into the air," he defended himself weakly.

"I'm surprised at you, Steven," Joe said, with disbelief in his voice. "Capp has no way of knowing that you weren't shooting to hit him. As bitter and angry as he is, what will happen now? What if he carries a loaded gun with him and seeks revenge? I wouldn't blame him at all.

"I'm really afraid that you've shot into a hornet's nest, or even worse. I'm afraid you've put us all into real danger."

Steven felt awful as Joe's words sank in. *It's true. Why hadn't I thought before I acted?* he thought. *What a foolhardy thing I've done!*

Joe's voice softened. "Jesus says we are to love our enemies and pray for those who persecute us. The Bible says we are to live in peace with all and do good to others. I'm afraid we've lost our chance with Capp. I don't know if any amount of love and goodwill we show to him will do any good now.

"Ya, well, what's done is done. Let's get back to bed. We'll ask God to forgive us and protect us."

Downstairs in the kitchen, Joe took care to lock all the doors. "I'm really worried now," he admitted to Arie. "I don't think Steven realized how bitter and angry Old Capp is. I guess he thought he's just a harmless old man who wanted a chicken or two."

Arie nodded. "It's just too bad. We'll have to do all we can to make amends."

Then she gasped. "What if Capp comes into our house tomorrow when we are in church and steals my cash box with the strawberry money? Maybe I could hide it under a bed. We can lock the doors, but none of the old windows have locks on them. Even if they stick, he could easily break a window and crawl in."

"He could do a lot more than steal a bit of cash," Joe replied. "He could set the buildings on fire or poison our food, since he already had food poisoning on his mind. But it's foolish to talk like that. Hide your cash, and let's trust God to protect us."

"Where can I hide it?" Arie wondered. "He might look under the bed, or— Oh! I have a good idea. I'll put the box inside the stove! He'd never think to look there." She got the stove lifter and raised a round lid. The wooden cash box fitted nicely inside. "There, that's safe until Monday," she declared.

Joe chuckled. "I'd never have thought of such a clever hiding place," he marveled. "Just so you don't forget it before you start a fire again."

"I won't," Arie promised.

Upstairs, a subdued boy crawled back into bed. Regrets and unease plagued his mind and made him feel awful. Now he understood the risk he had brought upon the household. What had possessed him to shoot the gun like that? Why, oh, why, did he do such a foolish thing?

Joe had really given him a going over. His bright idea had sure backfired. It was a long time before sleep overtook Steven again.

Over in Capp's shabby old house, the old man stood at the dirty cracked window for a long time, muttering to himself and peering out. His dog, Wuf, paced back and forth uneasily, growling occasionally, sensing his master's anxiety.

"I don't like it one bit, Old Pal," he said to the dog. "This shootin' in the night! Makes me think a body isn't safe in his own bed, next thing.

"People aren't to be trusted nowadays, no siree, they aren't. They're all out to get you, somehow or other. I don't trust anybody, and I never will again. I've been cheated and swindled. I've been taken!"

His voice rose to a shriek, and he clenched his fist and brought it down on the table with a crash. The dog whined and lifted his nose and began to howl mournfully. The sound seemed to bring Capp back to the present. He sank down on the rickety old chair with his head in his hands.

At last he walked wearily over to his cot and crawled into bed. His mattress was a thick layer of straw covered with old newspapers. The dog lay down on his floor mat. Soon the room was filled with the sound of snoring.

16

Sally and Andrew

SUNDAY morning dawned cloudy and cool. "This weather sure wakes us up, compared to the heat we had," Arie commented, as she and Joe went out together to see how the chickens had fared. They mounted the dusty stairs to the upstairs of the barn, Joe taking the lead.

"Well, well, the door is still latched," Joe noticed. "And the chickens seem to be all right."

Arie began to count the chickens through the wire mesh of their pen. "One, two, three, four, . . . sixteen. They're all here but two, I think." She counted them again. "Yes, there are sixteen left. Two are missing."

"Not bad!" Joe was surprised. "I hope Capp has a good chicken dinner today. Or maybe he wanted them for his dog." Together they went downstairs to do chores.

Steven and Nancy came into the barn, carrying pails of milk replacer prepared for the calves.

"*Gude Mariye* (good morning)!" Joe greeted them kindly. He wanted to show Steven that although he had talked quite sternly last night, he harbored no ill feelings.

To Steven, Joe added, "I hope you didn't feel too bad about what I said last night. Everything seems to be quiet and peaceful over at Capp's house this morning, with smoke curling out of his chimney and all the birds singing. And only two chickens are missing."

Steven smiled his thanks.

"You know," Arie said, "I've been thinking that maybe it wasn't even Old Capp that took those chickens. If it was a possum or some other critter, a good scare was just what he needed."

"Hey, that's something to look into," Joe agreed. "I never gave it a thought."

"I'm going to check it out right now," Steven said eagerly. It hadn't occurred to him either. As he ran up the stairs to the *Scheierdenn* (barn floor), he wondered why he hadn't thought about that possibility.

Steven went over to the back of the pen. Sure enough, the wire was loose at the bottom, and a few boards were broken in the barn wall. The loose feathers scattered around told the story.

He bent down to look closer. Was that a little track there in the dust? Steven swung himself down through the hay hole, landed on the edge of the feeding trough, and ran out the back door. There, just under the place where the barn boards were broken, lay a half-eaten chicken. All around it in the soft mud were little tracks that looked like tiny hand prints.

"Coon tracks!" Steven exclaimed aloud. He burst out laughing. "That makes me feel a lot better." He hurried around the barn to tell the others.

Joe whistled in amazement. "Ya, well, that just goes to show that you should never put the blame on anyone before you have proof. It sure is a relief to hear that it wasn't Capp. I'm real glad to hear it."

"Same here," Arie agreed. "It's a load off our minds. But now we'll have to hurry or we'll be late for church."

Steven hummed "*Das Lobleid* (the Praise Song)" as he went to his room to get ready. Nancy heard him from her room as she put on her *Halsduch* (cape) and *Schatz* (apron), and she joined in the singing.

A damp breeze blew in the window. She closed it, shivering as she did so. It was hard to believe that just yesterday they were wishing for relief from the heat, and now it was too cool to have the windows open.

Joe was hitching Chief to the *Dachwegli* (carriage), and Nancy hurried down the stairs and out the door. Arie was already there, fastening the traces on one side. "Church is at Sol Fishers today, and we have four or five miles to go, so we'd better get started," she said. "We don't want to be late."

"Sol Fisher?" Nancy asked. "Do you think they're related to the Fishers that are neighbors to Jacob and Mary? I got to know Sally and Andrew quite well when I was there last summer."

"They likely are," Arie replied. "Maybe you'll get to see them there."

Steven chuckled. "That Andrew, he sure is a character. I wouldn't mind talking with him again."

Church services were being held on the *Scheierdenn* (barn floor) of the Fishers' big bank barn. Rows of backless benches had been placed there, ready for the people to be seated.

Nancy eagerly scanned the group of girls waiting in the corner near the ladder to the haymow. If Sol Fishers were Sally's aunt and uncle, then there was a good chance Sally would be there even though this wasn't her church district.

A moment later someone tugged at Nancy's sleeve. She quickly turned, and there Sally was, her face wreathed in a welcoming smile.

"Nancy, I'm so glad to see you," she cried. "Mary told me that you are at Joe and Arie's place and that you would be here. Is it all right if Andrew and I come and visit you this afternoon at Joe's? He wants to see the chestnut ridge."

"Wonderful!" Nancy exclaimed, genuinely glad. "What time do you want to leave?"

"Andrew and I came in the carriage, so you and Steven can go with us. That way we can leave whenever we want to. We'll have more time that way."

"Sounds great!" Nancy beamed. "It's almost too good to be true."

There wasn't time to say much more before it was time to be seated. Nancy quickly glanced across the barn to the boys' side as they filed in. Sure enough! There was Andrew, walking with the boys, looking just a bit taller and older than when Nancy had seen him last.

I wonder if he's still the same nixnutzich (mischievous) chap, or if he's more grown-up now, she mused. *Andrew wouldn't seem like Andrew if he wasn't up to something.*

The *Vorsinger* (song leader) started the first hymn, his deep melodious voice rising and falling, singing solo until it was time for the others to start, too.

Nancy's eyes returned to Andrew, and she found that he was looking at her. Incredibly, his lips twitched with a suppressed smile, and he slowly and deliberately winked at her. Nancy blushed and looked away.

He's still the same Andrew. I'm sure of it now, she thought. She was a bit indignant, but secretly pleased. *The nerve of him!* And yet he looked so innocent and beguiling. For a while after that, she found it hard to keep her mind on the services.

She didn't look at him again for a long time. When she glanced again, his eyes were on the preacher and he seemed to be listening intently. *It's time I do the same,* Nancy scolded herself. *I should be ashamed of myself for getting flustered.*

As soon as the services were over, Nancy and Sally went over to the porch. The women were busy getting the food ready for the simple noon fellowship meal. Some of the men were helping to set up the tables. There would be homemade bread and rolls, smearcase (spreading cheese), *Rotriewe* (red beets), pickles, church spread (a mixture of peanut butter and molasses), *Schnitzboi* (dried-apple pie), coffee and tea.

The porch swing was still unoccupied, and the girls gratefully sank into it.

"You're going to be jealous when I tell you this, but I get to baby-sit a lot for your niece, Nancy Ann," Sally said. "She's a little sweetheart. Whenever Mary goes out to help Jacob in the barn and fields, I get the chance."

Nancy made a face. "It isn't fair, and I'm jealous. I wish they'd live next door to us."

Her face brightened. "At least I'll be seeing her nearly every day this coming week. Jacobs are coming over to help us get ready for the barn raising, and I'm staying till then."

Steven and Andrew sauntered by with the other boys in their age group, heading for the shade tree. "It looks like they hit it off right away," Sally observed. "At the rate they're talking away, they're probably two of a kind."

"Probably," Nancy agreed. "But remember, they did get to know each other before, that day that we raced with the deacon and the fifth wheel broke, and Andrew sprained his arm."

Sally giggled. "Oh, yes, and Andrew was chased up a tree by a dog. It was a good thing it was him that sprained his arm. It served him right for being so *grosshunsich* (smart-alecky)."

Steven turned and called to Nancy, "Be ready to

leave right after dinner. Andrew wants to drive out to see the chestnut ridge, and we're going along."

"That suits me," Nancy said happily. "I'm glad it's such a cool day, just right for hiking. Or maybe you'd rather do something else."

"Nope," Sally replied. "At least I want to see that strange old man's place that Mary was talking about. He must be something else."

After dinner the boys went to hitch the horse, and Nancy went to tell Arie about their plans.

"That's fine with me," Arie agreed. "We have an invitation to stay for supper, and if Joe's willing, we'll probably stay. You and Steven won't be afraid to be home alone this evening, will you? We'll start for home right after supper."

"Of course not," Nancy declared stoutly. "You can stay as long as you wish. Steven and I can milk the cow and take care of the other chores."

"Andrew's ready." Sally was at her side. "Let's go."

Out at the end of the walk, the boys were waiting with the horse. Sally and Nancy climbed in and sat on the backseat. The boys hopped in, too, and out the lane they went, the horse trotting at a fast clip.

"Is this the same *Esel* (mule) that ran away for you one time?" Steven asked, chuckling at the memory.

"It sure is," Sally piped up. "The same driver, too, only now he's a bit older and wiser."

Andrew promptly changed the subject. "Tell me all about the chestnut ridge and the wildlife."

The boys were interested in the same things and had a lot to talk about: wildlife, hunting, fishing, and trapping. Meanwhile, Nancy and Sally visited on the backseat.

As they approached the narrow bridge near Joe's farm, the horse stopped and snorted.

Sally made a face and whispered to Nancy, "Just watch him dump us into the creek. Wouldn't that be just like Andrew?" She rolled her eyes.

Nancy glanced down at the water churning over the rocks. "I'll get out and walk," she decided.

"Stay sitting," Andrew told her. "If I know my horse, I think he'll behave."

He got out and spoke kindly and reassuringly to the horse while leading him across. Once he swerved a bit, and Nancy stifled a scream. "That was too close to the edge for comfort!" But the next minute they were safely across.

"Well done," Steven said admiringly, and Nancy felt the same way. He had handled the horse well.

When they drove into the barnyard, Steven said enthusiastically, "First thing, we'll set a trap for the coons that are stealing Arie's chickens. Maybe we'll catch one tonight."

Andrew tied the horse by the barn. "What are you using for bait?"

"I think the half-eaten chicken would be as good as anything," Steven suggested. "There's a good chance they'll be back for it sometime, if they're hungry enough for chicken."

"You mean you're going to set traps on a Sunday?" Nancy scolded. But the boys were already disappearing behind the barn.

"Okay, let's take our bonnets into the house. Then we can head for the hills," she told Sally. "Do you enjoy bird-watching?"

"I sure do," Sally replied. "I wish I would've thought to bring my binoculars along."

"I'll let you use Joe's," Nancy offered. Knowing Sally, she had a feeling they would do more talking than anything else, and she was right. Sally was lively and fun to be with.

The afternoon passed quickly while they roamed the lovely surroundings and trails. Almost before they realized it, the sun dipped low and Sally and Andrew had to start for home.

"Brrr! It's getting really chilly," Sally said, shivering. "There's a big cloud blotting out the sun, and the east wind is *feicht* (damp). Next we'll have to close the storm front to go home."

Steven and Andrew had trudged all over the ridge, too, and were now back by the carriage. "Let's go before it rains," Andrew said briskly. "It's getting windy too."

"Good-bye, and thanks for coming," Nancy called to Sally. "Hug little Nancy Ann for me whenever you get the chance."

"I will," Sally promised. "See you at the frolic."

The horse started off with a will, and Andrew guided him in a circle around the water trough, then headed out the lane. He stuck his head out the carriage door and called back, grinning, "Good-bye. See you tomorrow."

Nancy stared blankly at Steven. "Tomorrow?" she asked. "Where will you see him tomorrow?"

"Right here," Steven said, smiling. "He's coming with Jacob and Mary to help put in the footer and lay blocks for the dairy barn. We need all the help we can get, and I asked him to come."

"Well!" Nancy sure was surprised.

17

Money to Burn

BACK in the kitchen, Steven flopped down on the rocker with the *Young Companion* magazine and began to read.

"What do you want for supper, tomato soup or strawberry soup?" Nancy asked him. "We'll probably have to eat alone since Joe and Arie are invited to stay at Sol Fishers for supper."

"Es macht nix aus." Steven shrugged his shoulders. "It doesn't make much difference to me, but you really ought to start a fire in the range. It sure feels chilly and damp in here. We'll probably get more rain soon."

"That would be a good job for you, Steven," Nancy told him. "You can do that while I make supper."

"Nah, that's woman's work," Steven protested. "I'm going out to sit on the porch to read. It's no cooler outside than it is in here." He took his magazine and went outside.

"Der faul Rumlaefer (the lazy bum)!" Nancy griped. "I wish Dad were here to make him do it." She went to the washhouse for the kerosene jug, and to her disgust found that it was empty.

At least I have the kindling that Capp so "generously" got ready, she thought gratefully. *Now I won't have to hunt for cobs.*

Nancy grabbed the empty jug and went out to the big tank beside the barn to fill it. She opened the spigot, and the kerosene ran into the jug in a slow trickle. "That will take at least a half-hour to fill," Nancy muttered impatiently. "Why don't I just get a tin can and take enough to start the fire? I can come out later when the jug is nearly full."

"Now be sure you don't burn the house down like Arie nearly did," Steven called from the porch.

In exasperation Nancy retorted, "If you want to be so helpful, keep your eye on that kerosene jug. Close the spigot when it's full, and don't let it overflow. That's your responsibility now."

"Hmmm, we'll see," Steven drawled.

Outside, Nancy poured the kerosene from the tin can over the kindling, put it in a cardboard box, carried it to the range. Next she got some newspapers to stuff into the stove.

What's this? she wondered when she lifted the stove lid. *A wooden box in the stove? Ya, well, I guess*

Arie wanted it burned or she wouldn't have put it in the stove. She stuffed the newspaper on top of the box, then laid the kindling. *Now, where are the matches?*

At Sol Fishers where church services had been held, Joe and Arie decided at the last minute to go home for supper after all. Joe took his rig to the yard gate, reined up Chief, and waited for Arie to climb into the carriage beside him.

"I don't think Steven will shoot into the air again," Joe said, "but it's hard telling what will happen yet, with Capp the way he is. I'm just not sure about Capp. I hope he's just a harmless old man, but I just don't know. He's mighty bitter, and it's hard telling what a crotchety old man could do in such a state of mind. He must have heard the shooting last night from his place."

"Ya, you're right," Arie agreed. "I guess it's best that we go home for supper and the evening. Anyhow, we can make sure the chores are done right. It sure would be nice to have good, trustworthy neighbors instead of a sour one like Capp."

Chief was peppy and eager to get home, trotting briskly all the way.

"It sure is nicer for the horses since it cooled off," Joe commented. "Such an early, unseasonable heat wave is hard on man and beast. No time to get used to it gradually."

As they drove in the lane at Chestnut Ridge Acres, Arie suddenly gasped. "*Was is letz* (what's wrong)?" Joe asked in alarm.

Arie was speechless. She pointed to the thin wisp of smoke coming from the chimney. Then she jumped from the carriage and ran for the house as fast as she could, her shawl flapping in the breeze.

"Nancy, Steven," she shrieked.

Nancy rushed out the kitchen door, and Steven jumped off the porch.

"Mach's Feier aus," Arie screamed. "Put out the fire!"

She ran into the kitchen, grabbed the bucket of drinking water, lifted the stove lid, and doused the fire with it. The stove hissed and released steam and smoke. In a wink Arie had dug under the kindling with a little coal shovel and lifted the money box from the stove. It was still burning. She fled to the yard with it and beat it with the porch mat.

"Mei Aebeer Geld (my strawberry money)!" she moaned. "Why did I hide it in the stove?"

Nancy gasped in dismay. Her heart sank when she realized what she had done. *"Ich hab des net gwisst* (I didn't know that)," she lamented. *"Unvergleichlich* (strange)!"

Arie pulled the half-burned paper money out of what remained of the box. Joe had tied Chief and came running to see what was wrong.

"Es Geld is verbrennt," Steven told him, disbelief in his voice. "The money is burned."

Joe took the box to the porch and used a little stick to dig the money out of it. "Some of these bills can be salvaged, I think," he said hopefully. "We'll take them to the bank. Maybe they can replace some of them.

135

Maybe it's not as bad as it looks. At any rate, it's just money."

He turned to Arie. "When I saw you running like that, I feared the worst. What a relief to see it's just burned money."

Arie laughed shakily. "I'm sure I looked ridiculous, but I thought if I ran fast enough, I could save the money. We worked hard to pick all those berries."

"I—I'm so sorry." Nancy felt crushed. "It was all my fault. I should have looked to see what was in the box before I put the kindling on top. I'll pay you back somehow even if it takes me five years."

"You'll do nothing of the sort," Arie declared. "I shouldn't have put the money box in the stove. Let's put this away now and forget about it. *So geht's wann's gute geht* (all's well that ends well)."

However, Nancy couldn't forget about it that easily. Her heart felt heavy as she crushed strawberries, added sugar, and put them into a bowl with bread cubes and milk for supper. *Next I'll be more trouble than I'm worth here,* she thought miserably. *That sure isn't a nice feeling.*

At the table the strawberry soup was absolutely tasteless to her. The kitchen was chilly, for no one had bothered to start another fire. *I'll repay Arie,* Nancy resolved. *Money can be replaced. It's not so bad—not like something lost forever.* Having resolved that, she began to feel better.

Thump, thump, thump. Someone was banging on the door! Joe jumped up from the table and opened the door. There stood Old Capp, peering in. "Kin I

have some more o' them strawberries?" he queried. "I kin chop some more wood for 'em."

"The nerve of him!" Arie declared, under her breath. "After trying to deceive us by turning the barrel upside down!"

"I'm sorry," Joe told Capp. "Today's Sunday, and we couldn't allow you to do that today. Come back tomorrow if you want more."

Capp spat on the ground. "You're mean," he whined. "First you take my land, and now you won't give me any more berries." His voice rose to a shriek, and he thumped his walking stick angrily on the ground.

Joe turned to Arie. "Do you have any more berries picked?"

"No, but you could offer him some of this strawberry soup. There's plenty left, and he could sit on the porch to eat it."

Joe nodded. "Fill a bowl, and I'll see if it suits him." He took the soup out to Capp and said pleasantly, "Here's a bowl of strawberry soup for you. You can sit on the porch rocker to eat it."

Capp's face softened when he saw it. "Strawberry soup," he murmured. "Just like Ma used to make." He took the bowl and spoon and sat on the edge of the porch.

Steven peeked out the window. "He looks like a happy little boy," he chuckled. "I'm going to take him a piece of cake, too." He put some cake on a saucer and also stuffed some bread crusts into his pocket for the dog.

"Make sure you don't tease him," Joe warned. "It doesn't take much to anger him."

"It doesn't take much to please him, either," Steven returned. "This cake ought to make him happy."

Out on the porch, Steven held out the cake to Capp. "Here's something for you," he said.

Capp glanced at it and grunted, but kept on eating, so Steven put the saucer on the porch beside Capp. In a flash Capp's dog jumped onto the porch and eagerly gobbled up the cake, wagging his tail. He looked up at Steven, his eyes begging for more.

Steven sat on the porch bench and threw a piece of bread crust to the dog, who caught it in midair and swallowed it in one gulp. The next piece he put on the bench beside him, and Wuf jumped up on the bench. When the pieces were all gone, he nuzzled around Steven's pockets, searching for more.

"Du bisht net en beeser Hund," he murmured, petting the dog. "You're not a mad dog. You're probably half starved." He went into the house for more scraps. When he came back out, Capp and his dog were already headed for home.

"Were you able to befriend the dog?" Arie asked when she came out on the porch to shake out the tablecloth.

"Sure thing." Steven nodded, enthusiastically. "All it took was something to eat. He won't make any trouble for me."

"Sel is gut (that's good)." Arie was glad to hear it. "I hope we can turn Capp friendly, too. Somehow, I think he's just a poor eccentric old man. It would be

so much nicer to be on friendly terms with him. He can be unpredictable when he's angry."

Steven and Joe went to the barn to milk the cow and feed the animals. Nancy and Arie washed and dried the dishes and put them away.

That night Nancy was getting ready for bed, thinking how much better it was to sleep in cool weather, when she could snuggle under a quilt. She heard a knock on the door.

"Nancy," Steven called softly, "did you turn the spigot shut on the kerosene tank?"

Nancy yanked open the door. "Steven Petersheim," she gasped, "don't tell me you didn't take care of that jug!"

"I didn't," Steven said miserably. "Do you think it's still running? I'm going out now to see."

Nancy followed him down the steps. "Let's sneak," Steven whispered. "Joe doesn't have to know."

Out at the tank, he shone the flashlight on the jug. "The jug is full," he said. Then, feeling the spigot, he added, "But the tank is empty. The spigot's wide open, but the kerosene is all."

"Oh, no," Nancy groaned. "I burned their money, and you drained the tank of kerosene. I wonder how full the tank was."

Steven shook his head sadly. *"Ach, mei Zeit* (oh, my), all that kerosene wasted. Feel how squishy the ground is around the tank. Ei yi yi."

"Dumm (stupid)!" Nancy exclaimed. "We'll have to be more careful. This has taught us a lesson, an expensive one, too. I think we should try to repay Joe, every penny."

"How do you plan for us to do that?" Steven wondered.

"I don't know yet, but I'll figure it out, and you've got to help me," Nancy declared. "It was your fault, too."

"I don't know what we can do to make some money."

"You must help to think of something." Nancy was close to tears.

"Well, all right, when the trapping season opens, I'll trap muskrats and give that money to Joes," he promised. "They're plentiful around here, and the last I heard, the pelts were worth $5 apiece."

"Thanks, Steven," Nancy sighed with relief. Maybe her brother wasn't as noncaring as he acted sometimes. "I'm so glad I can count on you to help."

"Go to bed now," Steven replied. "I'm going to check my raccoon trap first." He disappeared around the corner of the barn.

Nancy felt better as she walked to the house. A few wind clouds blew in front of the moon, and down at Capp's place a low, mournful howl drifted up on the wind. She shivered and began to run. That sound made her think of howling wolves, panthers crouched in trees, and bears prowling around. No midnight walks on the chestnut ridge for her!

18

Andrew the Tease

NANCY was dreaming. It was pitch dark. She was walking through the chestnut ridge, sneaking so the panthers, bears, and wolves wouldn't hear her. Danger lurked behind every tree and bush. Then from not far away came a fearsome howl. Nancy tried to run, but her legs wouldn't move. She tried to scream, but no sound came out.

The howling was getting fiercer and closer. Then bang! bang! bang! Nancy was suddenly wide awake, and she jumped out of bed. *"Was in de Welt* (what in the world)!" she exclaimed.

The banging was louder now, and the eerie howling continued. Through the window she saw faint streaks of dawn lighting the sky in the east, so she knew it must be early morning. She dressed as fast as she could, her heart pounding.

Steven came dashing out of his room just as Nancy was ready to go down the steps.

"What's going on?" he asked, looking about as scared as Nancy felt.

"That's what wonders me," Nancy said. "Let's go find out."

Joe and Arie hurried out of their bedroom into the kitchen just as Nancy and Steven raced down the stairs.

"Open the door," a voice yelled. They heard more heavy pounding. "Open this minute, I tell ya!" Bang, bang, bang!

"It's Capp," Arie said shakily. "He must be awful mad."

Joe opened the door cautiously and stepped back. "You're thieves, that's what you are," Capp yelled, shaking his fist and waving his walking stick. "You stole my dog, you dirty scoundrels. He's in the barn somewhere. I heard him howling out there. You give him back right now, or I'll call the cops, and I mean it."

"If your dog is in our barn, he went in by himself," Joe said, trying to sound calm. "We didn't pen him in."

"You lie!" shrieked Capp, poking his stick nearly in Joe's nose. "Go get him out now!"

Steven began to run toward the barn, and Capp quickly hobbled after him. "Yup, the boy knows something about it," he said triumphantly. "It was the boy, I just knew it."

Steven hurried around the barn, followed by the

others. Just as he had expected, there was Capp's dog with his foot caught in the coon trap.

"Poor boy," he said softly, kneeling to release the dog. Capp came up panting, yelling, "Get away, get away from my dog. I'll have you arrested, I surely will. Aha! You set a trap for him, that's what you did."

Both Steven and Joe tried to explain that the trap was set for a raccoon that had been stealing chickens, but Capp wouldn't listen. He kept on raving and ranting while he set the dog loose.

Capp stumbled off with the dog limping at his side. He kept on shouting back insults and threats until he was out of earshot.

"Whew, was he ever mad!" Joe exclaimed.

"I'm mad, too," Steven said angrily. "I'd like to kick his rear end. He knew we didn't trap his dog on purpose."

"Now, Steven," Joe reprimanded, "would that be turning the other cheek? Somehow we have to return good for evil. Let's think of something to make peace."

"Old Capp was nearly beside himself. I guess we can't blame him for being upset that his precious dog was caught. That dog is the only friend he has. Can't you set your trap inside the barn near the chicken pen after this?"

"I sure will," Steven declared. "I never once thought about it that the dog would come nosing around up here. Maybe he was hunting for something to eat."

"We'd better hurry and eat breakfast now," Arie said. "Next Jacob and Mary and more helpers will be here before we're done with the morning work and the washing."

"And Andrew," Steven added. "I can hardly wait to tell him what happened."

"You'd better tell Joe about the wasted kerosene," Nancy whispered to Steven. "Remember, I told you to close the spigot when the jug was full."

"Okay," Steven said meekly, feeling sorry now that he had sassed back to Nancy the evening before.

When Joe heard the story and Steven's offer to pay for the loss, he commented, "I'm more worried about the stuff soaking into the ground than I am about the money. It's a fifty-five-gallon drum. Since it was almost empty, we lost maybe ten dollars. But it pollutes the ground. What if it gets into our drinking water? We'll have to make sure we don't spill any more."

Nancy was pinning the last load of wash on the line when she spied Jacob's King prancing in the lane. Yes, there was Andrew on the front seat beside Jacob, and Mary and little Nancy Ann on the back seat. She hurried to the washhouse with the laundry basket, wanting to run out for Nancy Ann and yet feeling shy because of Andrew.

More helpers were arriving. Nancy quickly attached the hose to the washing machine and let the water drain out the back washhouse door. Then she went to meet Mary and to get Nancy Ann.

"We're so glad for your help today," Arie was saying. "The men will be pouring the footer for the dairy barn, and tomorrow they'll be laying blocks for the foundation. That means we'll have to cook for all the helpers. We have to get treats ready for midforenoon and midafternoon, too."

"I brought a big can of cookies," Mary said. "Maybe Nancy could gather plenty of mint in the meadow so we'll have lots of cold tea ready for the thirsty workers."

"Sure, and I'll take Nancy Ann along, if I may."

"She'd like that," Mary agreed. "Better put her bonnet back on. It's still cool. Be sure to stay away from Capp's place."

Steven had told Mary about Capp's latest visit before he and Andrew headed for the work site.

Nancy Ann eyed Nancy solemnly as she carried her along to the meadow. She was a cute baby, with dark eyes, round cheeks, and little bobbies (hair rolls) on each side of her head. "Today I have the chance to hold you, and Sally doesn't," Nancy said happily. "You're *my* niece, not hers."

The grass in the meadow was lush, green, and dotted with buttercups. "Pretty soon this meadow will be dotted with black and white cows," Nancy murmured to Nancy Ann. "We'd better pick all the tea we want before then."

She plucked all the stalks she could hold under one arm, with the baby on the other arm. Nancy rejoiced in the delightful fragrance of the mint and balsam tea. She was tempted to go for a walk along the creek, but she had to hurry back to help prepare dinner for the men.

In midafternoon Nancy took tea out to the workers, and Mary brought snacks for them. Andrew and Steven were helping to level off the concrete that had been poured in the forms to make the footer. They were so thirsty that each of them gulped down two cups of tea.

It was a short, busy day. When Jacob's party and the other helpers had left, Nancy could hardly believe her eyes when she saw Andrew coming in for supper with Steven and Joe.

"Don't look so surprised," Steven chuckled. "Jacob and Mary are coming back tomorrow, and Andrew was planning to come along again to help. So I just asked him to stay for the night. We want to go coon spotting after dark tonight on the chestnut ridge and maybe even sleep out on the ridge, too. It really warmed up again this afternoon."

"Just don't stay up too late," Joe warned them. "We want you to be worth something tomorrow for helping."

Then Joe turned to Arie and Nancy. "Well, this afternoon when I was in town to pick up some building supplies, I took the burned money to the bank. They were able to replace about two-thirds of it. Only about one hundred dollars was so completely destroyed that they couldn't replace it."

Joe explained to Andrew what had happened.

Nancy blushed. She wished no one else would find out about her *Dummheit* (stupidity), especially Andrew.

"It wasn't your fault, Nancy," Arie said consolingly. "I should never have hidden the money in the stove in the first place."

"Ya, well," Nancy said gratefully, "but I still plan to pay you back sometime. I'll earn the money somehow."

147

In a low voice so the others wouldn't hear, Andrew teased, "You could make *Gnepplin* (dumplings) to sell." He winked again.

Blushing, Nancy remembered what had happened when she was at Jacob's place last summer. She had burned the *Gnepplin,* and Andrew had spied her burying them. Now she just shrugged her shoulders toward Andrew and thought, *He's still the same character he always was, that's for sure. He'll probably never get over his love of teasing.*

19

Coon Spotting

"LET'S go," Steven urged. "We have our bedrolls, spotlights, and the grub for breakfast. What else would we need?"

"How about some matches to start the campfire?" Andrew suggested

"Ach, ya, and a few newspapers, too. Are you sure you put in enough for us for breakfast, Nancy?"

"Should be," Nancy said. "Make sure you don't break the eggs."

She watched as the boys trudged off into the velvety dusk, with fireflies flickering around them and frogs calling from the marshes. For a fleeting moment, Nancy wished she were a boy and could go along on their outing, to enjoy the excitement of sleeping on the ridge. Then she thought of panthers and bears and changed her mind.

The night was warm. As the boys trudged up the ridge, a soft breeze swayed the leaves of the chestnut trees overhead. In the distance a lone screech owl hooted eerily. Down by Capp's place, his dog howled mournfully. Thin clouds moved in front of the moon.

"Whew, this is going to be exciting," Andrew declared. "I just wish we'd have a good coonhound along to sniff 'em out."

"I wish we could've brought our guns," Steven complained. "I can't see why it wouldn't be all right to shoot them now, even though the season isn't open, since they're stealing our chickens. I'm peeved at Joe for not allowing it. If they keep on stealing chickens in spite of the traps we set, I'm going—"

A twig snapped behind Steven, and he whirled around. A dark form came out of the shadows, toward the boys, with yellow eyes gleaming.

"Wolf!" Andrew cried. He grabbed hold of a branch above his head and frantically swung himself up. Steven searched for a branch, too, but there was none nearby. For a moment he felt paralyzed with fear. He looked again when the animal was closer and shakily began to laugh.

"It's just Old Capp's dog, Wuf," he chortled. He snapped his fingers, and the dog came up close, wagging his tail.

Andrew sheepishly swung himself down from the tree. "He sure treed you that time, didn't he?" Steven couldn't resist rubbing it in, for he knew Andrew

150

would've done the same to him. He patted Wuf's head and scratched his ears. "You're not a wolf. You're just a friendly old *Hund* (dog), aren't you? I sure hope you can sniff out coons."

"Ya, he sure fooled me that time." Andrew laughed at himself. "Ya, well, let's go see if he can tree the coons, too."

As it turned out, Wuf was an excellent coon dog. He was none the worse for having been caught in a trap, with no aftereffects except a slight limp. In no time at all, the boys had a furry masked creature in the beam of their spotlights, and then a short time later, another. The third was in a tree not far from Capp's place.

"What's that strange noise I hear?" Andrew wondered. "Sounds like someone sawing wood, far off."

"Let's sneak closer to Capp's house," Steven suggested. "Maybe it's him, snoring."

That was exactly what it was. Under the tree beside his house, Capp lay rolled up in a blanket, with his feet sticking out at the bottom, snoring vigorously. The boys quickly dropped to the ground, helpless with laughter but trying to suppress it.

Between spasms, Andrew said, "With all the noise he's making, it's no wonder he didn't hear his dog baying." Then he added eagerly, "Hey, let's have a bit of fun with him. He'd never know who did it."

"Like what did you have in mind?" Steven asked curiously.

"Well, we could loosely tie his legs together, then throw stones onto the roof of his house and run for dear life," Andrew chuckled. "It would serve him right for getting so mean and angry and accusing you of stealing when his dog was caught in your trap."

"Yes, it would. We ought to do something." Then he paused, remembering that Joe and Arie were hoping to win Capp's friendship and be on good terms with him. They wanted to return good for evil.

Steven's conscience pricked him, but he just wanted to have a bit of fun with Andrew. He didn't want to play a mean trick on the poor old man, just a harmless prank.

He told Andrew, "It can't be anything really bad. We don't want to get him so angry that he'll seek revenge. Maybe we can do something harmless like carrying that bench out into his yard."

"Say!" Andrew began to laugh. "I've thought of just the thing. Let's set his bench right over top of him, then set a bucket of water on top of the bench. When he sits up, the bench will overturn and the bucket of water will dump over him. Ha, ha! He'll have a surprise bath then!"

"Wow, where do you get your clever ideas?" Steven said in admiration. "That's just what we'll do. But we ought to do something to scare him yet, so he jumps up real fast. If he sleeps until the sun comes up, he'll see the bench and crawl out from under it slowly."

"Hey, that's a great idea," Andrew exclaimed, shaking in anticipation. "Now you're the one with the bright ideas. We'll throw some rocks on the roof, then run and hide, just like I said."

"Why don't we wait to scare him until tomorrow

morning, just before dawn," Steven suggested. "Then we'd be able to see it better."

Actually, Steven was afraid their night of sleeping out would be spoiled, with an angry man on their trail.

"Suits me," Andrew nodded. "Let's get that bench there now, though."

The boys sneaked over to the house, and each took hold of an end of the bench. Capp's snoring was as loud as ever. Wuf was still out in the woods, sniffing out rabbit trails. Tiptoeing over, the boys placed the bench over Capp, with the legs on either side of him.

"Now for a bucket," Andrew whispered.

Steven shone his spotlight in through the open kitchen door. There against the wall, just a few feet from the door, stood a bucket. Andrew reached in and got it. "There's a few inches of water in. It's too bad it's not full," he whispered. "We can bring more water along from the creek when we come back before daylight. Ya, well, let's get to our beds, then."

The boys headed back up the ridge to where they had left their supplies. They crawled into their bedrolls and lay there, dreamily talking about anything from fishing, trapping, and deer hunting to having their own horses and buggies, *rumschpringing* (running around with the youth group), and dating. Finally they grew drowsy and fell silent.

The night was enchantingly mellow and misty, with soft, fragrant breezes stirring gently, stars twinkling overhead, and a pale silvery moon peeking down through the tree branches. The chorus of the frogs and night insects lulled them to slumberland.

Suddenly Steven was wide awake. What had he heard? Something, some animal, was following their trail, coming toward them silently, except for the stirring of the underbrush and the creaking of the grasses. He felt his hair stand on end. He expected a bobcat to pounce on him any moment. He lay tensed, ready to spring up.

Then there was Wuf, wagging his tail and happy to be with the boys again. "You buster," Steven said fondly, with a sigh of relief. "This is the second time tonight you scared me. Good dog. You want to sleep with us, don't you? You like us better than grouchy Old Capp, huh? Lie down now and go to sleep."

As if the dog could understand, he curled up between the boys, with his head

resting on his paws. Andrew was already asleep, according to his deep, even breathing, but sleeping seemed to be out of the question for Steven for a while. His scare had made him too wide awake.

His thoughts turned to Capp. *Is it right for us to do that to the poor old man?* he wondered. Bible verses chased each other through his mind: "Do unto others as you would have them do unto you. . . . Return good for evil, and pray for those who persecute you. . . . Live peaceably with all people. . . . If your enemies are hungry, feed them."

Steven felt ashamed that he had agreed with a plan to tease Capp. What would Andrew think if he changed his mind now? Would he think him a weakling or a sissy? But what would Joe and Arie think if he was partner in such a prank?

Finally he made up his mind. *Es macht nix aus was Andrew denkt,* Steven decided then and there. *It doesn't matter what Andrew thinks. I'm going to persuade him to help me remove the bench and bucket of water instead of scaring Capp by throwing rocks.*

After he decided that, he felt better and happily snuggled down into the bedroll, listening to the pleasant sounds of woodland and meadows. He peacefully drifted off to sleep, dreaming of the wonders of nature and wildlife and the enchantment of the woods.

When Steven woke up the next morning, Andrew had already built a campfire in a circle of stones, with the frying pan on top. He was frying mush for breakfast. Wuf was hungrily eyeing the grub and wagging his tail.

"Wake up, you *Schlofkopp* (sleepyhead)," Andrew teased. *"Zeit die Kieh melke* (time to milk the cows) The sun will soon be up. Get the plate for the mush, and then I want to put the eggs into the pan."

Steven stretched himself and yawned. He got up lazily, wondering how he was going to tell Andrew that he had changed his mind about teasing Capp.

Then Andrew spoke up. "You know," he said half sheepishly, "I've been doing some thinking. That was mean of me to suggest that we play an unkind joke on Capp. I've got a better idea. Why don't we fill a plate with mush and eggs for Capp and take it over to him now, and take that bench and bucket away. It's early enough that he should still be fast asleep."

Steven laughed in relief. "That's a good idea," he agreed. "It would be more like heaping coals of fire on his head than a prank. If your enemies hunger, feed them."

"I'm going to eat a plateful myself first, though," Andrew declared. "My stomach is growling, and I'm powerful hungry. It's a good thing Nancy put in enough for Capp and Wuf, too."

"I'm hungry, too," Steven agreed. "But we'd better hurry or Capp will wake up before we get there."

Providence must have been smiling on the boys. When they came to Capp's clearing with the plate of mush and eggs in the predawn light, the old man was still sawing wood as heartily as before. They quickly returned the bucket to its place and removed the bench.

In their haste, they happened to nip Capp's leg

157

with one of the bench brackets, and the snoring suddenly stopped. The bench was just barely in its place when Capp sat up, blinking his eyes as if in a daze. "What's going on?" he asked gruffly.

"We brought you some breakfast," Steven said, in his friendliest voice. "Mush and eggs." He held out the plate to Capp.

For a long moment, Capp stared at the plate. Then, to the boys' embarrassment, tears filled his eyes.

"Mush and eggs," he repeated, "just like Ma used to make." Tears ran down his wrinkled old cheeks, and his shoulders shook.

"Let's go," Andrew urged.

As the boys started across the clearing, Capp called after them, "Thank ya, boys. I'm much obliged."

"Wow!" Steven exclaimed. "That's the nicest he ever talked. What if we'd have done what we were planning to? I'm mighty glad we didn't."

"Same here," Andrew said gruffly. "He sure was pleased."

20

Treasure in the Garden

ON Wednesday morning when Mrs. Shprecher came to pick up her berries, she walked over to look at Arie's garden. "My, your garden is clean!" she exclaimed. "It's beautiful, the rows are so straight, and there's not even a weed in sight, not one."

"Thanks to Nancy's help," Arie said, smiling. "But I'm sure you could find a dozen weeds if you looked close enough. I don't know what I'd do without her help, what with cooking for the workers, picking peas and berries, and keeping after the weeds and all."

Mrs. Shprecher sighed. "I'd sure like to have Nancy for a few hours to help me in my garden sometime. I'm so busy in the store, and the weeds are taking over. But I sure don't want to take her away from you when you're so busy. Maybe after your barn raising is over . . ."

"Hmmm! Nancy is planning to leave for home with her parents in the evening after the barn raising." Arie was pondering. "But I'll tell you what. Several of our church women are coming along with their men to help me today. I feel sure I could spare Nancy for a few hours tonight if that would suit you. It will be nice and cool then to work outside."

"That would be great!" Mrs. Shprecher said happily. She walked over to where Nancy was weeding a flower bed. "Would you like to help me in my garden for a few hours tonight?" she asked.

"Sure." Nancy was willing.

"All right, then, I'll come for you after supper. My husband, Fred, used to work in the garden a lot, but since he's been gone these two years I think sometimes I should give up having a garden. It's just too much for me. But I'd sure miss the fresh vegetables out of the garden."

After they loaded boxes of berries in the back of her pickup, Mrs. Schprecher got in and leaned out the window. "See you tonight at around six," she called to Nancy, waving her hand.

Nancy waved back. "Mrs. Shprecher is nice," she told Mary, "even though she doesn't wear a *Kapp* (head covering). It'll be fun working for her."

That evening promptly at six, Mrs. Shprecher came driving in the lane at Chestnut Ridge Acres in her old truck. Nancy hurried upstairs to put on a clean *Schatz* (apron). In a few minutes, she was seated beside the friendly old lady on the seat of the pickup. Nancy slammed the door, but not quite hard enough for it to latch.

"Try again," Mrs. Shprecher said kindly. On her third slam, Nancy finally had it latched. *My, this pick-up is battered, compared to the Baileys' car,* Nancy thought. She had done some cleaning for them when she was at Jacob's place for the summer. *It doesn't have air conditioning, either.*

Mrs. Shprecher's home was nothing elegant, either, compared to the Baileys' mansion. It was just an old-fashioned weather-beaten white frame house. There was a friendly back porch attached, and roses rambled over a trellis. The back screen door was just like the one on the back porch at Chestnut Ridge Acres. A plump, friendly, three-colored cat sat on the porch steps.

"We've lived here for fifty years," Mrs. Shprecher explained. "Gardening used to be my hobby, but now that I'm old and stiff, I can't do as much anymore."

Mrs. Shprecher opened the woodshed door and beckoned Nancy to follow. She selected a hoe, shovel, and rake, and directed Nancy to push out the wheelbarrow.

There was an old-fashioned, white picket fence around the garden. When Mrs. Shprecher pushed open the gate and Nancy got a glimpse of the garden, she was pleasantly surprised. "Oh, it's beautiful," she exclaimed in wonder.

A profusion of sweet peas, wild roses, and old-fashioned petunias tangled over each other all around it, and in one corner various kinds of herbs were thriving. Here and there were little patches of vegetables, with a garden path winding among them.

An old stone birdbath stood in the middle of the flowers. At the end of the path was a picturesque stone garden bench. A sundial in the center of the garden gave it a quaint look.

Nancy was delighted. True, it was weedy and unkempt, but it was also enchanting.

"I love this old garden," she told Mrs. Shprecher. "It's much nicer than if everything were neat and prim."

Mrs. Shprecher chuckled. "I'm glad you like it. Fred and I spent many a pleasant evening in here, but working alone isn't as much fun."

She began to prune and clip, while Nancy chopped with the hoe, stopping to pull the bigger weeds by hand. Mrs. Shprecher kept up a friendly conversation, and the time passed quickly. After an hour of working, she straightened up and declared, "I say it's time for a break. Let's go into the house for iced tea and a snack."

At the kitchen table, she placed a plate with a piece of luscious-looking chocolate cake and a glass of iced tea in front of Nancy, and cut a piece for herself. Nancy was thirsty, and she took a sip of the tea, wondering if it was mint or balsam. She nearly sputtered. It sure wasn't good old meadow tea.

Glancing at the counter, she spied a canister of tea mix. *That explains it,* she thought. *I've never drunk that kind before, so no wonder it tastes strange.* She took a forkful of chocolate cake.

"Mmm, it's delicious," she declared. "About the best I've ever tasted."

"It's one of my specialties." Mrs. Shprecher beamed proudly. "Fred used to say there's no one who can make chocolate cakes like I can."

Just as Nancy was ready to take another mouthful, something caught her eye. She stared in disbelief. There, on her piece of cake, nearly invisible to the human eye, were tiny red ants crawling around on it. They were almost exactly the color of the cake. Mrs. Shprecher was eating her piece with gusto.

Nancy looked closely at her piece and, yes, it had tiny ants on it, too. She watched as Mrs. Shprecher's last bite of cake disappeared into her mouth.

Now I'm in a predicament, Nancy thought in dismay. *If only I could secretly smuggle my cake into my pocket somehow. What can I do? It would embarrass Mrs. Shprecher terribly if I'd tell her about the ants. I can't say I don't want it either.*

She looked around wildly. There was no way out of it. Bravely she put another forkful of cake into her mouth, quickly grabbed her glass of tea, and took a huge swallow to wash down the cake. Then another, and another, forcing herself to swallow. At last only a few crumbs remained. Nancy rinsed her mouth with the last of her tea and gulped.

There, I did it! she gloated to herself. *Those ants won't hurt me, I know.*

"Now, you rest as long as you like," Mrs. Shprecher

said kindly. "I think I've done enough for tonight. Do you mind working alone?"

"Oh, no, I don't mind a bit," Nancy assured her. "I'll get right back to work now."

Back to the garden she went. For another hour she hoed vigorously, trying not to think of those ants. Finally Mrs. Shprecher came outside again. "It's time to quit now, Nancy," she called. "You've done enough for tonight."

"But I'm nearly done," Nancy protested. "I'd sure like to finish it yet before I go."

"My, you're a fast worker!" the old lady gushed as she sat down on the garden bench. "It does my heart good to see you and my clean garden. I'm so pleased with the work you did."

"Thank you," Nancy said politely. She swung her hoe to chop out a big weed. The hoe didn't dislodge the weed, so Nancy bent over and pulled with both hands. Slowly but surely it was coming. She braced herself so she wouldn't fall.

There! She knocked the dirt off the roots and tossed the giant weed into the wheelbarrow. A tiny glitter at her feet caught her eye, and she bent to pick it up. It was an old finger ring, covered with dirt.

"What's that you have there?" Mrs. Shprecher asked curiously.

Nancy took the ring to her. She examined it close-ly, then gasped. "My engagement ring," she ex-claimed. "Why, I just can't believe it. I lost this nearly fifty years ago."

For a while Mrs. Shprecher just sat there, looking

dazed. Then to Nancy's embarrassment, she began to cry. A minute later she was laughing. "Oh, Nancy," she said shakily, "you have no idea how much this means to me. It has a diamond in it, but the sentimental value of it is much greater.

"Oh, I wish Fred were here to see that the lost ring is found. When the children were small, we promised a reward of a hundred dollars to whoever found the ring. They spent many an hour digging around for it, but never with any luck."

Suddenly she jumped up from the bench. "You shall have the hundred dollars," she declared. "I have that much in the house now, and I'm going to get it for you."

Nancy was flabbergasted. She watched Mrs. Shprecher hurry to the house. *A hundred-dollar reward?* Of course, she wouldn't accept it. Nancy tried to call Mrs. Shprecher back, but she didn't seem to hear.

The hoeing was soon done, and Nancy sat down on the bench. *It wouldn't be right to accept it,* she decided. But Nancy hadn't reckoned on Mrs. Shprecher's insistence. She simply refused to take no for an answer. When they started for home in the pickup, the money was in Nancy's pocket.

Nancy was awestruck. She had never had so much money before. She began to dream of all she could buy with it. Mrs. Shprecher kept exclaiming over the found ring, saying how glad she was, and thanking Nancy over and over.

They were nearly home when Nancy thought about

165

the money she had promised Arie to replace the strawberry earnings that were burned. For a few moments, she felt disappointed that the money wouldn't be hers, but then she realized that it was an answer to prayer. She was cheered by the thought that she could help Arie and they could put that episode behind them.

When Mrs. Shprecher stopped in front of the house at Chestnut Ridge Acres, Nancy got out of the truck. Mrs. Shprecher called out, "Your hard work paid off tonight, didn't it?"

"It surely did," Nancy agreed. "I can't thank you enough for what you gave me." She waved as Mrs. Shprecher drove off. With a chuckle she said to herself, "It was even worth eating those ants for that amount."

21

The Frolic

THE day of the barn-raising frolic finally arrived. Nancy awoke to the rumble of thunder and bright flashes of lightning in the still dark sky. Rain splashed on the porch roof, and she quickly closed her window.

"It's too bad, just when we were hoping so much for a nice day," she murmured as she got dressed. "Oh, well, *so geht's* (so it goes)."

Arie had breakfast on the table when Nancy came into the kitchen.

"What are you planning to do, postpone the frolic?" Steven asked Joe as he seated himself at the table. "Do you think the van loads from back home could come another time?"

"Oh, we'll go ahead with it," Joe assured him. "Dads are probably on their way out now already. This storm will likely blow over soon. But we may get another storm tonight. The old saying usually holds true: If there's a thunderstorm in the morning, there'll be another in the evening."

While they were bowing their heads for silent grace, there was a bright flash of lightning followed by a loud clap of thunder.

"Whew!" Arie exclaimed, after they had raised their heads. "I'm sure glad the electricity has been taken out of this house. I've heard say that lightning can follow the wires. I hope the storm doesn't come any closer."

She passed the plate of mush, ponhaws (scrapple), and eggs to Steven, but he sighed and passed the plate to Nancy without taking any.

"What's wrong, Steven?" Joe asked, concerned. "Aren't you feeling well?"

Steven sighed again. "I was hoping you'd postpone the frolic," he said dejectedly. "I have a terrific toothache, and it really hurts."

"That's too bad," Arie said sympathetically. "When were you last at the dentist's office?"

"I've never been there yet," Steven admitted

"Never?" Arie's eyebrows went up.

Steven shook his head.

"I hadn't gone to the dentist yet at that age either," Joe told her. "Not till I was eighteen, and then I didn't have any cavities."

After breakfast Joe turned to Steven. "Let me look

at that tooth that hurts. It's dim in here on account of the storm, so I'll get a flashlight." He shone the light into Steven's mouth.

"It's a large cavity, all right," he declared. "It looks like the other teeth are crowding that one out, too. It's protruding out the side where it doesn't belong, and it's higher than the others. I don't have time to take you to the dentist today, but I think I could pull it for you if you want me to. Then the other teeth would have the room they need, too."

"*Was in de Welt* (what in the world)!" Arie was aghast. "What would you use? And what if it would bleed a lot?"

Joe was confident that it would be all right. "I have a small pliers," he said, "and he can stuff some cotton into the empty space. I don't think it would bleed much. Are you game, Steven?"

"Anything to be rid of this pain," Steven groaned. "I don't think the hurt of having it pulled could be much worse than what I feel right now. The sooner it's out, the better."

"Well, I declare!" Arie shook her head and walked off. "I'm sure not going to watch. But be sure to rinse out your mouth with peroxide, then, to prevent an infection. I'll boil some water to sterilize the pliers."

"I'm not going to watch either," Nancy said emphatically. "I sure wouldn't let anyone but a dentist pull my tooth." The storm was abating, and she began to wash the breakfast dishes.

When Joe had the pliers ready, Steven closed his eyes and opened his mouth. He braced himself for the pain. It was all he could do to keep from yelling when Joe yanked and twisted the pliers.

After what seemed like a long time, Joe cried triumphantly, "There, it's out! The roots are intact, too. Wasn't that a neat job! I think I'd like to be a dentist."

Steven ran for the wash basin and grabbed the cotton.

"You poor boy," Arie said comfortingly. "Here's some Tylenol for your pain. You won't need to work today if you don't feel like it."

True to Joe's prediction, the storm soon did blow over. Before long, dozens of men began to arrive in trottin' buggies, two-wheeled carts, and spring wagons. Some brought their families in market wagons and carriages. The vans from their home community arrived, too, and it was so good to see Mamm, Daed, Susie, Lydia, and the boys again.

The women were soon bustling around, busy with food preparation. They were getting drinks and treats ready to set outside on tables at midmorning for the men.

Nancy was helping with the potato peeling, and the task seemed endless. She kept watching the door, hoping to see her friend Sally soon. Then finally she was there, beckoning to Nancy at the door, just as they were peeling the last of the potatoes.

"Let's go and watch the men for a while," Sally suggested. "The way it looks, there are enough women here that we won't need to help until it's time to set out the refreshments."

"Listen to all that hammering," Nancy marveled.

"It's hard to believe that by tonight the dairy barn will stand."

Rows of framework sections were ready and waiting on the ground. The excitement began as the frames were raised one by one. The men used ropes and poles to push and tug them upright. They were fitted into place and fastened there.

Nancy spied Andrew silhouetted daringly against the sky, working with the men. Steven had apparently opted to stay on the ground because of his sore mouth. The girls sat and watched in fascination until a voice called from the house, "Come on, girls, we need your help to make sandwiches."

Hurrying back inside, Nancy and Sally were soon busy slicing cheese and bologna and spreading butter or mayonnaise on the bread slices. Bowls of fresh Buttercrunch lettuce out of the garden stood ready, and the sandwiches were assembled in a short time.

"I don't think it will take much coffee and hot chocolate today," Arie decided. "Cold meadow tea and lemonade will go better when it's so warm and muggy. The weather's not settled yet, and if it doesn't give another thundershower before nightfall, I miss my guess."

"Ya, well, we're just thankful it's not pouring down rain on the workmen now," Mamm said.

Nancy and Sally helped carry the cupcakes and doughnuts out to the tables set up in the yard. Others brought the prepared sandwiches and gallons and gallons of drink.

"Your job will be pouring the drink into the paper

cups," Arie told the girls. "See to it that the men don't run out of drink. The way they're sweating, it's going to take a lot."

Joe motioned for the workers to stop and take a break. It didn't take much coaxing. The workers were mostly Amish, joined by local farmers and visitors. The girls were kept busy pouring tea and lemonade, but they could catch some of the men's conversations at the same time.

"You mean you pulled Steven's tooth for him?" a young married Amishman asked Joe.

"Sure did," Joe said, a bit proudly. "It sure beats paying a dentist."

"I should say so," the man marveled. "I have a tooth that needs to be pulled, too. If you're so good at it, I'll just come over here to have it done."

"Fine with me. It won't cost you a cent," Joe offered generously. "Come over sometime after the cows are in and we're not so busy anymore."

"Hey, I have a tooth that needs pulling too," someone else spoke up. "When can I come?"

"Now wait a minute," Dad spoke up in protest. "Didn't you hear about that man in Mifflin County? He pulled teeth for other Amish people, and he got fined for practicing unlicensed dentistry."

There was a silence among the men, then one of them spoke up, "I don't think the officials would find it out."

Dad shook his head. "Whether or not the officials find it out has nothing to do with it. We want to obey the laws of the land, not just when someone is watch-

ing, but all the time. There's someone above who sees all we do."

"I guess you're right," Joe said meekly. "I hadn't thought about that. I won't pull any more teeth."

The group of men went back to work, and the girls' next job was carrying what was left back into the house. Then three long tables were set up under the shade trees, ready to be set for dinner. Tubs of water and towels were put out on the lawn where the men would gratefully wash the sweat and grime from their faces and arms.

Nancy and Sally had a little break to watch the progress at the dairy barn. Soon it was time for them to help make the *gschtammde Grummbiere* (mashed potatoes) and dish up steaming platters of fried chicken, bowls of gravy, fresh peas out of the garden, homemade noodles, and lettuce salad.

For dessert there were puddings and jams, shoofly pies, cherry pies, and *Yuddekaschboi* (ground-cherry pies). The Amish believe in setting a bountiful feast for their workers. For several hours over dinnertime, the girls were kept busy filling and refilling dishes, clearing and resetting tables, and washing dishes.

"At last," Sally said with a sigh of relief, when the last dish was being wiped. "Let's find us each a *schnuck Buppeli* (cute baby) and sit down somewhere."

"All babies are *schnuck*," Nancy said, "but I know which one I want."

"Nancy Ann, of course." Sally laughed. "I think I'll get myself a little boy."

They went outside with their little charges and sat on the overturned washtubs under the shade tree.

"I wish Lakisha, the Fresh-Air girl, were here," Nancy said wistfully. "Will she be coming again this year?"

"She's planning to," Sally nodded. "She and Tyler both, in a few weeks."

"But I'll be back at Whispering Brook Farm by then," Nancy sighed. "I'm going along home today, and it spites me that I won't get to see her."

The girls spent their free time talking a mile a minute, playing with their babies, and watching the workmen. "*Guck mol datt* (look there once)," Sally motioned toward Capp's place.

The old man stood by his barn, watching the workmen on the emerging dairy barn. "Maybe he never saw the likes of this before."

"Probably not," Nancy agreed. "I wonder what he thinks of all this commotion. Hey, we should've invited him to come up for dinner."

"Ya, well, it's too late now," Sally said. "It's already about time to begin setting out the afternoon refreshments."

The rest of the day passed quickly. All too soon the van was there to take the Petersheim family home. Nancy and Sally sorrowfully said their good-byes under the shade tree, promising to write to each other.

Arie thanked Nancy for coming to help and pressed a twenty-dollar bill into her hand as they parted.

Once inside the van, Nancy realized how much she

was going to miss Joe and Arie and Steven, and even the chestnut ridge. "Good-bye, Chestnut Ridge Acres," she mouthed the words. "Someday I'll come back to live on the chestnut ridge. I'll buy an acre of land from Joe and build myself an old-maid house back there. It is one of the most beautiful spots I've ever seen."

Outside by the barn, something caught Nancy's attention. It was Andrew, waving his arm in farewell. She wasn't sure whether he was waving to her or someone else, but she waved to him anyway. *Good-bye, Chestnut Ridge Acres,* she thought. *Precious memories!*

22

An Angry Bull

FINALLY the day came when the new dairy barn was ready for the herd of cows. Joe was in a high state of excitement, rushing around doing some last-minute things before the big truckloads of cows would arrive. The new milking machines were all ready on the racks in the just-completed milk house, and the bulk tank had been installed and hooked up.

"Only one small job to do yet," Joe sighed. He dragged the portable air compressor over to the milk house to power the drill. "I have a few bottom holes to drill yet for the lower hinges on the milk-house door."

Alas, the old maxim, "Haste makes waste" proved to be true for Joe. As he bent his head in concentration, there was a whirring sound, then a sharp pain in his chin. "My beard," Joe yelled. He shut off the drill and ran for the house, holding his chin with his handkerchief.

"Was in die Welt (what in the world)!" Arie gasped, seeing the remains of poor Joe's beard. "What happened?"

Joe headed for the mirror that hung above the wash basin. "Oh, no," he groaned. He closed his eyes in disbelief. Half of his beard was gone. *"Unvergleichlich* (weird)," he groaned. "Get me the scissors," he called to Arie. "I can't walk around like this."

"Oh, your beautiful beard!" Arie lamented, as she brought the scissors and a bottle of peroxide.

Joe snipped off the remainder of his beard, then grinned weakly. "I guess I forgot I had a beard," he said sheepishly. "I was just *huddlich* (too hasty). Now I'll have to shave the whole thing off as soon as I'm able and start growing it again."

Arie smiled and teased, "It'll be nice to see you again looking like my charming beau."

Steven came running in from the barn. "The cattle trucks are here," he called excitedly. "They're stopped down by the narrow bridge, and I don't think they trust crossing it."

Joe's beard was forgotten in this next predicament. Steven and Joe jumped on big-wheeled scooters and kicked their way down the lane to size up the situation. *"Elend* (misery)!" Joe muttered. "What will go wrong next?"

He wanted to put the cows into the barn for their first milking before putting them out on pasture. Now the only thing to do was to open the fence near the trucks and herd them into the meadow. Joe hoped they'd be willing to come into the barn nicely when it was time to feed and milk them.

Joe took the rails out of the fence. With the help of Steven and the two drivers, one by one the thirty Holstein cows were chased through the fence. The one driver kept yelling, "Hya, hya, hup, hup," and the other one shouted, "Hya, phub, hya, phub," much to Joe's amusement, but it seemed to help get the job done.

"Nice cows," the one driver remarked. "Now just the master of the herd to unload yet."

Joe's heart sank. He had forgotten about the bull. He peered into the truck, and his heart sank still further. The bull was huge and angry looking, with his head down, pawing the floor of the truck. If only there were a way to put him into the strong, safe bull pen in the barn instead of in the meadow.

The thought of putting such a powerful brute into the meadow made Joe uneasy. Since there was no other way, he reluctantly told the driver to open the bull's compartment and chase him out. For a few anxious moments, Joe thought the bull was going to slip by them and run off down the road. Just in time, he swerved and ran into the meadow among the cows.

Joe quickly put the fence rails back in place. "So far, so good," he muttered anxiously. "Now if only the meadow fence holds him properly."

The bull was in an ornery mood. With his head down, he began pawing the ground and bellowing in a threatening way. Then, still snorting, he lifted his head and stared at an object far back in the meadow.

"Oh, no," Joe gasped. To his horror, he saw Old Capp ambling across the far end of the meadow, with his dog scouting around him. Capp was unaware of any danger.

In a flash, the powerful beast was off with a surprising amount of speed for his size, heading straight for Capp. The onlookers could do nothing but watch in helpless horror. There was no time to help Capp. Joe's arms dropped limply to his sides. He stood petrified with dread. He couldn't stand to watch, yet his eyes were locked on the unfolding drama.

Not till Capp heard the thundering of hooves did he turn. Then he saw the powerful, angry bull coming at him. With a wild, shrill scream of fear, he began to run. In a moment the monster was almost at his heels, bellowing and shaking the earth beneath him.

However, Capp's dog, sizing up the situation and seeing his master's danger, sprang up with lightning speed. He sank his fangs into the soft part of the bull's nose and swerved him to the side just as he had moved in to attack the man.

With a roar of pain, the bull tried to attack the dog, but Wuf was too quick for him. Then with another lightning-quick dash, he again sank his fangs into the bull's nose from the other side. Thus he distracted the bull, attacking again and again, until Capp had time to run to the fence and roll underneath it to safety.

Next Wuf bit the bull in the tail and held on. The brute circled angrily, trying to reach the hateful creature that was causing him so much pain. Finally he gave it up. With a fierce bellow of rage, he took off at top speed in the direction of the barn.

Arie had been watching the whole terrifying drama from the barnyard. She quickly opened the heavy iron door to the bull pen and then retreated to safety.

To the relief of all, the bull ran into the pen and stayed there, guarded by Wuf, whose fangs he had learned to respect. Joe came running and slammed and locked the door.

"Are you sure it's wise to keep such a dangerous creature on the farm?" Arie asked in concern. "I don't like it at all."

"Definitely not," Joe declared emphatically. "If I'd have it to do over, I'd never even have unloaded him. We don't need that kind of a bull around. He has got to go."

The day turned out to be a hectic one. Getting the cows into the barn and then to the proper stanchions was a frustrating job. Being at a new place made them nervous. When milking time rolled around, Joe felt as tense as the cows.

On top of all this stress, in the middle of milking, Old Capp came into the dairy barn, angrier than they had ever seen him before—absolutely livid with rage.

"What do you mean by turning your bull on me?" he roared. "I'm going to get even with you, you just wait and see. I'll get my revenge." He was trembling in his fit of rage. "I'll set fire to your barn, I'll shoot all the cows, I'll put a stick of dynamite under the whole place." He stamped his foot with each threat, seeming to grow angrier and louder each time.

Then he quieted and said, deadly serious, "I mean it. I'm not just kidding. I'll do what I say." He turned and walked out of the barn.

It was the last straw for Joe. The outburst had frightened the cows, and two had kicked off their milkers and lunged back and forth. It was just too much. Joe was a grown man, but he wanted to cry. His chin ached from having his beard torn off. His cows were upset. His neighbor was threatening him. What more could go wrong today?

He wished he had never seen the Chestnut Ridge Acres farm and the herd of cows. Wearily he trudged over to fix the cows' milkers and was rewarded by a kick on the shin. It seemed like an awful long time until the day was finally over, and Joe and Arie crawled into bed.

Soon Arie was asleep, but Joe was too exhausted to settle down. Whenever he dozed off, he dreamed he was falling and took a big leap, which jerked the bed. Sometimes he dreamed that his beard was being yanked off.

Finally, after several hours of this, he fell asleep. He dreamed of chasing the cows and the angry bull. Then the bull was after him. "Hyah, hyah, hup, hup," he yelled excitedly.

He tried to grab hold of the bull's tail, but instead he grabbed Arie's hair bob and shook it so vigorously that the hairpins flew out. "Hyah, hyah, hup, hup," he shouted again.

Arie loosened his hold on her hair and jumped out of bed. "Joe, what's wrong?" she cried in alarm.

Joe sat up in bed and blinked. "The bull's after me."

Arie burst out laughing. "You just had a nightmare," she giggled, getting back into bed. *"Danki Gott* (thank God) that not all days are as stressful as this one was. *Ball wollt's besser geh* (soon it will go better)."

23

The Hawk

THE next day was busy, too. At the supper table, Steven said wistfully, "I'd sure like to go fishing sometime when we're not so busy anymore. After the shower we had again this afternoon, the night crawlers should be out. It wouldn't be hard to get bait."

"I'll give you time off tomorrow," Joe promised. "I want you to take the gun sometime, too, to hunt groundhogs. Just the other day I noticed some freshly dug holes. I don't want a horse to step in one and break a leg when we're cultivating corn."

"Stay away from Capp's place," Arie warned. "As angry as he was last night, it's hard telling what he'll do. I just wish we'd have a decent neighbor instead of such an unpredictable one."

"I think it was just idle threats," Joe said. "I sure wish that scare hadn't happened with the bull, and I don't blame him for being upset. We sure ought to give a reward to that dog of his. He's quite a gem and deserves a medal of valor."

"I'll say," Steven agreed. "I wouldn't mind having a good dog like that."

As soon as the evening milking and the other chores were done, Steven got an old tin can and filled it half full of dirt. Then, whistling, he walked out into the yard. The velvety dusk was descending and fire-flies were flickering. The fragrance of moist earth, summer grasses, and flowers mingled with the barn-yard smell of the cows as they slowly ambled out to pasture.

A moment later a friendly form with a wagging tail appeared out of the mists. "Good boy!" Steven was glad to see Wuf, and he fondly scratched his ears. "If you're so good at attacking bulls, maybe you can help me find night crawlers, too."

Wuf whined and wagged his tail still harder. Steven shone the flashlight around over the moist earth. There was an earthworm! He pounced fast. "Gotcha!" he gloated. He knew they could disappear fast, espe-cially if one end was still in the ground. A moment later he heard Wuf whining. Wuf was wagging his tail and had a night crawler dangling from his mouth.

"Why, you smart dog!" Steven praised in astonish-ment. "I'd never have thought you'd know what I want." He took the night crawler from Wuf and put it into the tin can. Wuf ran off again and a few minutes later came back with another.

"Unvergleichlich! Du bisht shmaert (strange! You're smart)," Steven marveled. "This sure is easy." In a few minutes he had all the bait he needed.

Next morning right after the milking and breakfast, Steven set off for the hills with his fishing pole and bait, and the rifle. He wished Wuf could come along, but he knew Capp wouldn't allow it if he knew it. The birds were singing joyously from the trees everywhere. The world seemed to sparkle and shine from the washing it had received.

Steven whistled a happy tune. Fishing and hunting were his favorite pastimes, and today he had his chance. Arie had packed a lunch for him. His *Schnappsack* (knapsack) was full of sandwiches, apples, and a half-gallon plastic jug of water. Joe had told him he needn't be back until one o'clock. A whole four hours of luxury!

He decided to fish first, then hunt the groundhogs later. He set the gun against a tree, took off his strawhat, and baited his hook with one of the night crawlers. Then he cast his line into the water and leaned back against a log. Steven basked in the beauty of his surroundings and patiently waited for the nibble of a big trout. He knew there were plenty in the stream; he'd seen them jumping out of the water.

A movement on a slope some 150 feet away caught Steven's eye. A handsome ringneck pheasant came into view. The sheen of its bright ring of brilliant colors on the neck made it noticeable.

"Wow!" Steven exclaimed in awe. "I wish this were October and the pheasant season were open. That's a real trophy! I hope nothing happens to it before then."

A moment later a speck in the sky caught his attention. He gazed up into the blue sky, trying to figure out what the speck was. It was gliding gracefully in a circle. Each turn brought it a little lower, yet it seemed to be soaring on a breeze.

"It's a large bird of some sort," Steven decided. "Why, it's a *Hinkelvoi* (chicken hawk)!" He watched fascinated as the hawk circled, getting closer and closer to the earth. Suddenly it began to dive straight down, fast, its talons extended. The unwary pheasant had no chance. The hawk was upon it in an instant, killing it with its claws and beak, then flying up into a nearby tree with its prey.

"Ach, Yammer, sell schpitt mich (oh, trouble, that spites me)," Steven muttered in disgust. "That dirty scoundrel. I feel like shooting that thief. He had no right to kill that ringneck."

Steven reached for his gun with one hand and into his pocket for the cartridges with the other.

"Don't shoot! A hawk is a protected bird, and it's against the law," warned the voice of conscience within him. *"Ich geb nix drum* (I don't care about that)," Steven declared stubbornly. "No one will know anyway."

He quickly stuffed the cartridges into the gun. He hoped the hawk wouldn't see him and fly away before he had a chance to shoot. For a few moments Steven wavered, undecided and arguing with his conscience while the hawk tore into the pheasant, relishing his feast. The sight of it angered Steven, and he slowly raised the gun.

"You deserve to be killed," he muttered. He pulled the trigger, and **Boom**! The roar of the gun shattered the peace of the countryside. The sound vibrated and echoed across the hills and valley. The hawk tumbled to the ground in a flurry of feathers.

Steven quickly crossed the creek and ran over to it. At once Steven was filled with remorse and shame. The hawk was big, with a wide wingspan, a fine specimen. "It was only doing what it had to do to survive," he muttered guiltily. "Why did it make me so angry? Ya, well, I'll bury the bird, and no one will ever know."

He went back to his fishing and soon had three fine trout. His groundhog hunting went well, too. He shot two of them, so the fields would be safer for Joe's horses.

"I wish I'd have a shovel with me to bury the hawk," Steven murmured. "I'll feel better once it's out of sight."

An idea popped into his mind. *Why don't I just stuff it down the groundhog hole and cover it with dirt?* So he quickly disposed of the hawk and rolled a large rock on top, too. "There!" he said aloud with a sigh of satisfaction. "Now my folly is covered."

Steven sat down on a rock by the creek to eat his lunch, but somehow the shine had gone out of his day. He knew he had done wrong, impulsively and foolishly. The verse "Be sure your sin will find you out" kept churning through his mind, but Steven cast it off. "Huh!" he scoffed. "No one will ever know." Yet he felt uneasy and decided to head for home.

The next day, Steven was found out. Joe and Arie had gone visiting. Steven was mowing the yard when a late-model car came driving over the narrow bridge and in the lane. Two distinguished-looking men got out and came over to Steven.

Hmmmm, I wonder what these big shots want, Steven thought. *I hope they're not salesmen.*

"Hello," the one said, extending his hand. "Do you, by any chance, happen to know whether a hawk has been seen in this area within the last few days?"

Steven felt his face redden, and he lowered his eyes. He kicked at a stone, studying for a way out of his predicament. He couldn't think of any. Without looking up, he answered, "Yes, I saw one the other day." He knew that the guilt written on his face betrayed him.

Not unkindly, the man asked, "Do you know whether the hawk has been killed?"

Steven wanted to run off, or at least to change the subject and somehow squirm out of answering. He was trapped, and he knew it. Miserably, he nodded his head.

"Did you, by any chance, have anything to do with it?" the man asked.

There was no way out of it. "Yes, I shot it," he finally admitted in a low, barely audible voice.

"Where is the hawk now?"

Steven pointed toward the chestnut ridge. "Back

there, under the ground in a woodchuck hole with a rock on top."

The other man whipped out a pen and writing pad and took down Steven's name and address and both his dad's and Joe's names.

"I'm sorry, but there's a stiff penalty for shooting a hawk," he stated matter-of-factly. "They're federally protected birds. The guy that shoots one is lucky if he doesn't have to do jail time. Now, if you don't mind, we'll go look for the hawk. We'll be back to tell you what's what."

Steven watched as the men headed for the ridge, carrying a small shovel. "They'll never find it," he scoffed in amazement. "They didn't even ask in what area of the ridge it is." But in a surprisingly short time, they were back with the hawk. They put it into a plastic bag in the trunk and left.

Steven stared after the car in disbelief. "How in the world did they find it so fast?" he marveled. "Ei yi yi, I can't believe it. If only they would never come back." But deep down, he knew they would, and his guilt and the consequences hung over him like a cloud.

24

The Penalty

ARIE hurried with the feeding of the calves. She wanted to get her wash on the line as soon as she was finished with her chores. Then she would head for the fencerows to pick wild raspberries. They were plentiful this year, and she didn't want any to go to waste. Joe's dad was there helping for the day. She wanted to have a fresh raspberry shortcake ready for dinner.

A calf let fly with its heels, and Arie quickly jumped aside so that it just missed her skirt. "Why, you naughty *Hammli* (calf)," she scolded. "Here I'm all ready to give you your grain mix, and you treat me like that."

Finished with the chores, she hurried to the house,

scanning the skies worriedly. They didn't look promising for a good laundry-drying day. *"Sunne blicke, Rege dichte* (when sun is blear, rain is near)," she sighed. "Oh, well, maybe it will hold off until the wash is dry. We sure are having plenty of rainfall this summer. But we can be thankful for good growing weather."

Right after breakfast, Arie went into the washhouse to fill the wringer washing machine with hot water. It was so handy to just fasten a hose to the faucet and have hot water running into the washer from the gas water heater. That was better than having to fill a furnace kettle with water, build a fire underneath it, and dip the hot water into the washer. There was no furnace kettle here, not even a furnace, so there was no other choice.

Joe came into the washhouse. "Ready to have the engine started?" he asked. "Dad and I are about to install the horse-drawn barn cleaner."

"Yes, thank you." Arie beamed in appreciation. It was hard work for her to start the engine by herself. She was pleased that Joe had thought of it before he went out. After a few kicks on the starter pedal, the engine roared to life. It looked so easy when Joe did it, but for her it took much longer.

Arie sang as she put the clothes into the hot water, then through the wringer into the rinse water. Outside, while hanging the laundry on the line, she viewed the finished dairy barn with a feeling of satisfaction.

All that work was behind them now, and things

were going more smoothly. True, they were feeling bad about what Steven had done and what the consequences might be. But Dad felt confident that it wouldn't be worse than a hefty fine, and he would pay that.

"If only our troubles with Capp were over, too," Arie sighed. "I guess we'll just have to keep on praying about it."

An hour later Arie was headed for the fencerows with her plastic pails. The sun was out again. She hoped it would last a while and give the laundry a chance to dry. She stopped at the sweet-corn patch, hoping to find some ears ready.

"Ach, my," she gasped in dismay. Some of the stalks were broken down and stripped of their ears, a sorry sight indeed. "Coon damage! Oh, dear. Ya, well, we'll have to bring some dirty shirts and pants out here and set them up on sticks, like scarecrows. I've heard that the human scent keeps them away. I'll tell Steven to do that tonight."

Down by the fencerow, Arie was happy to see that the vines were laden with the purple jewels she was after. They were thorny and overgrown, but the berries were worth getting one's arms scratched up a bit.

A robin cheerily sang from the hedgerow, and a wren trilled from a nearby tree. *According to the birds, the world's running over with joy,* she thought. *They must love these raspberries as much as we do.* She went happily from bush to bush, not realizing how close she was getting to Capp's place.

Suddenly Capp's door flew open. He began to shout and yell at her, waving his arms angrily. "Get off my land," he screamed. "Git out! Git out!"

Arie hastily retreated. She had been careful to stay on their own property, but apparently Capp had different ideas. He kept on yelling and shouting until he was hoarse.

The world's certainly not running over with joy for Capp, Arie thought sadly as she went further up the ridge for berries. *With his heart so filled with bitterness, how can it be otherwise? What can we do to help him? Give him the land that he thinks belongs to him?*

Arie pondered this, the joy gone out of her morning. When her buckets were filled, she headed for the house

Back at the barn, Dad, Joe, and Steven worked side by side. Last night Steven had endured hours of tossing and turning, tortured by guilt and thoughts of the inevitable punishment. This morning he had confessed with the whole story of how he had shot the protected hawk. But what was done was done.

He had told it to Daed, who sadly shook his head. "Haven't I raised you better than that? I've taught you to obey hunting laws. You thought no one would find it out, but *der Heiland* (the Savior) sees everything we do."

He was grieved that his son had disobeyed. "No matter what wrong we do, we must face the consequences."

Steven hung his head at the memory. He knew he had deserved the lecture, every word of it. Dad had asked, "Do you think it would be fair of me to ask you to pay the fine yourself, even though it would take you until you're of age?" Steven had to admit that it would be fair.

That very afternoon a car again wended its way up the Chestnut Ridge Acres lane, and the federal officers got out. It didn't take them long to do their business. When they left, Steven Petersheim had been fined as much as a horse was worth. Dad had paid it for now, but Steven knew it was up to him to pay Dad back.

"Be sure your sin will find you out" is certainly true, he thought ruefully. *I hope I've learned my lesson.* He wished he could find something really valuable, like the ring Nancy had found, but he knew it wasn't likely. He would have to work hard to earn the money to repay his father.

The warden had explained that the hawk carried a radio-tracking device on its leg, so its whereabouts and habits could be tracked by a radio receiver with a directional antenna. That was why its death was discovered so quickly and they could find it so easily.

Steven found it hard to understand how such a thing could be possible, but he had to believe it. He was sure he would never again do anything against the law as long as he lived.

Later that afternoon, as Arie was in the kitchen canning raspberries, she noticed big drops of rain beginning to splash down. "My wash," she cried. "I must hurry and get it. It's nearly dry, and if I don't bring it in fast, it'll get wet again."

Arie slipped into Joe's light jacket hanging behind

the stove and rushed out with the clothes basket. She had a slightly sore throat and didn't want to get wet in the rain for fear it would turn into something worse.

As fast as she could, she grabbed the laundry off the line, throwing the clothespins into the basket. In her haste, she even stuffed a few small items of laundry into the jacket pocket when she wasn't close to the basket.

Joe came to her aid when he saw her rushing around. *"Dummle dich* (hurry)!" he teased.

"I'm hurrying," Arie returned, laughing. "I appreciate your help, though."

Then, as suddenly as it had started, the shower was over. It had lasted only a few minutes.

"You look cute in that jacket," Joe said. "I can't believe how much too big it is for you."

Arie slipped out of the jacket. "It was made to fit a big man," she teased. "I grabbed the first thing I could find when it began to rain."

"Dad and I are driving to town in the trottin' buggy," Joe told her. "We're going to the bank. I have to borrow money for the cows, and Dad has to sign the note. I don't think the rain will amount to much, but I'll take my jacket with me in case it starts to pour. Steven will stay here with you in case Capp makes you any trouble."

"Thanks," Arie replied. "Hurry back."

The next rain shower held off until Dad and Joe had reached the bank and were ready to tie the horse. Then it began to pour again. Joe flung his jacket across his shoulders, and Dad used the umbrella as they dashed across the parking lot and into the bank.

Seated in front of the loan officer's desk, Joe reached into his jacket pocket for a handkerchief to wipe the raindrops off his face. A moment later he wondered why the loan officer was grinning so. *I guess he's wondering what happened to my beard,* Joe thought.

However, Dad was staring, too, and his face was awfully red. He pointed to Joe's "handkerchief." For a bewildered moment, Joe stared too. Then, hot with embarrassment, he stuffed the offending item back into his pocket. It was a piece of woman's underwear!

That evening, when Joe told Arie about it, she laughed until the tears flowed. "Remember, I wore your jacket to bring in the wash," she reminded him. "In my haste, I stuffed some things in the pockets."

"Don't ever do it again!" he growled, pretending to still be angry but beginning to see the hilarity of the situation, too.

"So geht's wann's gute gehts (so it goes when it goes well)," Arie teased. "It does a person good to have a laugh like that every once in a while."

"Not when it's at your own expense," he protested. But he had to laugh with the others.

25

The Storm

THE midmorning sun beat down warmly as Joe guided the workhorses through the rows of healthy green corn. With the ample rainfall this summer, both the corn and the weeds were growing rapidly.

In the field next to the ridge, Steven was cultivating corn with the other team of horses. At the far end of the row, Joe spied Arie waiting for him with a pitcher of something to drink. His heart warmed at the sight of her. She was a partner in the truest sense of the word, as fine a wife as any man could wish for.

Without her and her cheerful *"Ball wollt's besser geb* (soon it will go better)," he would never have survived those hectic days, with all their ups and downs. Sometimes everything seemed to go wrong.

He felt confident that together and with help from above, they could weather the storms of life and make a go of farming here at Chestnut Ridge Acres.

At the end of the row, Arie met him with a question. "When are you going to do something about getting rid of that bull? He was raising quite a ruckus when I passed the barn on the way out here, bellowing and snorting. I'd feel a lot better if he'd be far from this farm, or turned into hamburger patties."

Joe drank a whole cup of fresh cold meadow tea before he replied. "You're right. I've pushed that off long enough now. I'd feel easier, too, if he'd be gone.

"He's raising Cain because he'd like to be with the cows, but he won't have the chance. At dinnertime I'll send Steven into town to ask the local cattle hauler to pick him up as soon as possible, maybe even today yet, to take him to the auction." Then Joe drank another cup of tea.

The arrangements were made. At two o'clock the old rattletrap cattle truck pulled up to the barn at Chestnut Ridge Acres. The driver tooted his horn impatiently. Joe had just come in from the field with his team and the cultivator, so he was on hand to help load the bull.

"Are you sure that truck can hold a big rambunctious bull?" Joe asked the driver. To him it didn't look like much more than a pickup truck with a wooden fence built around the bed.

"Sure, it'll hold 'im," the driver grunted. "I've hauled many a bull on this truck."

He backed up to the loading chute. After much

prodding and clubbing through the bars, the bull finally, with a bellow of rage, sprang onto the truck. Joe quickly clanged the tailgate shut.

After Joe paid the driver, he stood watching with some concern as the truck went slowly out the lane. The bull was restless. On seeing the cows in the meadow, he reared up on his hind legs and launched his front end over the side.

Joe gasped with horror. For a moment he thought truck and all was going to roll over onto its side. Slowly the bull went beyond a balance, hanging over the side of the truck for a few moments. Then with a creaking and splintering of wood and more bellowing, the beast tumbled into the ditch, rolled over a few times, and got to his feet, shaking his head in bewilderment.

Without wasting another minute, Joe headed for the barn to saddle Chief. Somehow the bull would have to be herded back into his pen as soon as possible, before he produced more *Dummheit* (stupidity).

Arie's heart sank in dismay as she watched from the kitchen window. "Oh, for closer Amish neighbors!" she lamented. "We do need help."

The bull was trying to get into the meadow to the cows, but the fence was electric. Again and again the bull bawled in rage as he was shocked while pressing against the wire.

Joe opened the barn door wide. Then, while riding Chief, he circled the bull. The driver of the truck had backed up close to the bull. With his help, Joe slowly drove the bull close to the open barn door.

Maybe this isn't going to be so bad after all, Joe thought. He began to breathe easier. *One thing is sure, if we ever get him back into his pen, he'll be shot. I guess we can butcher a beef here on the farm, even in this warm weather.*

However, the next thing he knew, the bull was running across the field, straight toward Capp's buildings. Joe's heart sank. Not to Capp again! He sat on Chief, looking dejectedly after the bull, trying to decide what to do. *What a mess!* he thought.

The truck driver seemed to be surly. "I guess it's your problem," he said shortly. "I have to be on my way, but I'll be back with a bill for the damages."

Now Joe felt like crying for sure.

Arie came out to stand beside Joe and the horse. "Where's Steven?" she asked anxiously.

"Cultivating corn in the south field. I sure am beat out with that bull. I wish he'd fall over dead with a heart attack."

A moment later the door of Capp's house opened. Wuf, a streak of fury, fearlessly descended on the bull. The bull saw his enemy that had caused him such pain and frustration when he first arrived at the farm. He turned tail and ran, heading for the chestnut ridge. A few minutes later, he disappeared from sight among the trees and over the ridge.

"Good riddance," Joe sighed. "But he's sure to be back soon. He'll try to jump the fence and join the cows. Maybe he'll come into the barn with them then. Meanwhile, I'm going to ride over to Capp's place to make sure he knows that the bull is loose."

"See how dark the sky is getting," Arie noticed. "It seems like there's a storm on the way."

Joe scanned the skies. "It sure does," he agreed. "That black cloud came up fast and without much warning. I was hoping we'd get the cultivating finished before it rains again."

By the time Joe reached Capp's house, big drops of rain had begun to fall, and thunder rumbled in the west. Steven was headed for the barn with his team, much to Arie's relief.

Joe dismounted and was ready to tap on Capp's door when it was flung open. Capp stood there, angrily glaring at Joe. Beside him was Wuf, wagging his tail.

"Git out," Capp yelled. "Yer tryin' to kill me with that bull, that's what you're doin'!"

Joe tried to explain, but it was no use. Capp was yelling and couldn't hear a word Joe said. Sadly, Joe turned away.

As he rode home, one jagged streak of lightning after another parted the clouds, and thunder followed. "Whew, this one came up fast!" Joe exclaimed. "That means it will be a bad one. When it rains, it pours."

He was also thinking of his troubles. But as soon as the words were spoken, the rain began to pound down in earnest, and Joe had to chuckle in spite of himself. He quickly put Chief into the barn and made a dash for the house.

They all stood at the windows, watching the rain and lightning. "We're having more than our share of hard thunderstorms this summer," Arie remarked.

"Maybe the storms are always worse here by the chestnut ridge."

"Look there!" Steven cried with glee. "Here comes the bull, running down from the ridge! The storm brought him back. He's trying to jump the fence into the meadow. Maybe the electric fence was grounded by the storm."

With another leap, he had crashed over the fence and was off to join the cows, who were huddled in small groups under the trees. "Aha, just what I hoped he'd do," Joe said. "Now he'll come in with the cows tonight."

The rain stopped abruptly, and the sky turned an ominous yellowish pink. Each thunderclap seemed to be closer, and the lightning more bright and intense.

Arie shivered. There was a strange feeling in the air that she didn't like, almost as if her hair were standing on end. *I wonder if the others notice it, too,* she thought.

The storm was so close now that there was no time between the flash and the sound. **Boom!** Arie jumped, then threw herself down on the settee. The next thing she knew, Joe was yelling, "The barn's been struck! It must've been the barn."

Suddenly the sky turned nearly as dark as night, and the wind roared and shrieked with a will. "Run for the cellar!" Joe yelled. "It must be a tornado!"

Arie ran blindly and yanked open the cellar door. Before they were halfway down the steps, the noise began to fade away. "It's over already," Joe said, with a sigh of relief.

"Are you all right?" Arie asked shakily. "It must've been a bad windstorm, if not a real tornado."

They sat together on the settee and the chairs as the thunder and lightning receded and the storm moved away.

"Now to check on the barn," Joe said. "If it wasn't struck, it was mighty close."

26

Under the Rubble

JOE could hardly believe his eyes when he stepped out on the porch. He blinked to make sure he was seeing right. Arie, coming out the door behind him, gasped in dismay. Steven whistled in disbelief. Where Capp's home had been, there was only a pile of rubble, heaps of old boards and roofing.

Along the fencerow, several trees were down, too. In a daze, Joe stared at it for a moment, then headed for the barn. Steven vaulted over the fence into the meadow, then excitedly began to call for Joe.

Joe wasted no time in getting there, and Arie was right after him. Just behind the barn, a big tree had been struck by lightning, split right down the middle. Under the tree lay four dead cows. Joe blinked his eyes to make sure he saw right. Yes, it was true; the bull was dead, too.

Just like that, killed in the twinkling of an eye. Joe felt guilty for having wished him dead. The other cows were still huddled under the trees, but alive. Joe shook his head to clear his thoughts.

"Joe!" Arie cried, her eyes like frightened orbs. "Do you think Capp was killed when his house crashed? Or maybe he's trapped under the rubble and badly hurt!"

With an exclamation of horror, Joe said, "We'll have to go search for him. He had to be in his house when it went down."

Together the three hurried toward the catastrophe, keeping to the fencerow to avoid the mud. They dreaded the thought of what they might find. At the edge of the pile of debris, Joe stopped and lifted his hand. "Listen! I think I heard someone yelling."

There it was again. "Help! Help! Get me outa here!" Wuf was barking frantically from somewhere, too.

"It's Capp! Let's try to lift these boards." They worked frantically, tense and frightened, hoping to find Capp, yet not wanting to see him hurt. It seemed as if they weren't getting anywhere. Arie finally declared, "This is no use. We must get help."

"Help is on the way!" Steven pointed to the road where a car had stopped. In a short time, someone was there with a tractor and front-end loader. Soon the rescue squad and an ambulance were there, too. A large crowd of people gathered, both helpers and onlookers.

Capp and Wuf were in the basement. When the last board was removed, a cheer went up from the crowd as they were pulled up to safety. They were frightened but unhurt.

Joe walked over to Capp. "You're welcome to stay with us," he kindly offered. "Then we'll help you rebuild your house."

Capp was still in shock, but he shook his head. "Thank ya," he said gruffly. "I'll sleep in my barn, in the haymow."

When it was time for the evening milking, Capp with his dog came up to the barn, though, and sat on a hay bale, staring sadly into space. He seemed much subdued, a completely different man.

Steven tried to strike up a friendly conversation with him. "Four less cows to milk. Come here, and I'll show you what happened." He motioned to the open door at the back of the barn.

Capp slowly got up and shuffled after Steven. His mouth dropped open when he saw the dead bull and the four cows. "You won't have to worry about that bull anymore," Steven said to him. "He'll never bother you again."

"So youns had a loss, too," Capp exclaimed. He seemed relieved to know that he had company in his misery.

The dead cattle were not fit for humans to butcher and eat since they had not been bled immediately after being struck down. Someone had called the scavenger truck. As they watched, it came in the lane and through the gate into the meadow.

A worker fastened a cable to the bull's rear legs. Then with a winch, he slowly and steadily pulled the bull up into the truck. He did the same with the dead cows. The carcasses would be used for pet food.

Wuf barked and tried to snap at the bull, disappointed that there was no response. In a split second, the powerful beast had been stripped of his power and fury and had gone the way of all flesh.

"It serves the ornery critter right," Capp muttered. "I'm sure glad he's dead."

Steven thought of the hawk. He, too, had decided that the hawk deserved to die, when it was just doing what its instincts told it to do. He felt sorry for the bull and the four cows.

Besides, it was an immense loss for Joe, when he was just starting out as a dairyman and trying to make a go of it. But it was better this way than if a human being had been hurt.

Capp declared that he wasn't hungry and refused to come into the house for supper. However, when Steven took a plate of food out to him on the porch, he did eat a little.

After supper, Joe walked with Capp and Wuf back to the ruins of Capp's house. Joe felt sorry for the bewildered old man and tried to think of something that would cheer him up.

In a moment of inspiration, Joe decided to ask Capp about the boundary-line dispute. He had been curious about it for a long time, but never before had he dared to ask. Now that Capp was so subdued, it might be a good time to ask.

"Say, Capp," he began, trying to sound nonchalant, "could you tell me where you think the boundary line between our properties ought to be? Maybe we could come to an agreement."

For a few moments, Joe thought he had been foolish to bring it up. Immediately Capp became agitated and aggressive, waving his arms.

"I'll tell you," he shouted. "See that big rock over there? That's where the boundary line is, not where the fencerow is. That's where my property ends."

Joe studied the situation. "Why, that's only a distance of about five feet for the length of the field. Why, that's not even worth arguing over. I'll let you have that."

Capp's eyes bulged. "Let me have it?" he repeated in astonishment.

"Sure," Joe told him. "I have no problem with that. Life's too short to be bitter over a property line."

Capp suddenly relaxed, like a taut rubber band gone flaccid. He leaned weakly against a tree, his shoulders shaking. "I was so bitter that Myrna couldn't stand it anymore. She left me and wouldn't come back," he moaned. "It wasn't worth it."

He walked away from Joe, with his head bent, stumbling over boards in his path as he went into his weather-beaten old barn.

"Come over to our place for breakfast," Joe called after him.

Capp just grunted in response.

As he turned and walked back home, Joe murmured to himself, "That poor old man. He was holding onto that grudge for so long. If he can't have that anymore, he's probably more confused than ever. Ya, well, at least we can help clean up the rubble here and see that a new cottage is built. I don't know what else we can do for him."

News of the storm damage spread throughout the Amish community. Jacob organized a cleanup crew for the next morning, for he knew of Capp's plight and his bitterness. By that evening, it was all nicely cleaned up. A pile of rubbish was heaped in the field, ready to be burned when the fire marshal gave permission and a fire truck was standing by.

Then Capp was gone for a few days. When he came back, he seemed like a different man. He had a haircut and was neatly dressed. The sullen, bitter look was gone from his face. He informed Joe that he was planning to rebuild and asked about an Amish carpenter crew.

Joe promised to get a crew for him, to organize the help, and to plan a frolic to put up the house. He promised to see to it that meals would be provided for the workers.

Capp thanked him profusely. When he had left, Joe said to Arie, "Capp is not as eccentric as we thought he was. Why, he's quite a decent and sane man, now that his bitterness is gone."

Arie agreed. "Isn't it amazing what an unforgiving spirit can do to a person!" she marveled. "If only he could have realized sooner how much harm he was doing to himself. He could have spared himself so much misery. All those wasted years of bitterness!"

27

Gratitude

ARIE stood at the kitchen sink, washing dishes, gazing out the window, and longing to be outdoors on such a gorgeous day. "Why, the leaves are changing color already," she noticed. "My, this summer just flew by. We were working so hard we hardly had time to enjoy it."

She glanced across the field and meadow, down to the neat little white bungalow where Capp's old shabby weather-beaten house had once stood. "It's hard to believe that it's all finished now," she murmured. "But our people sure helped out a lot. They attended as many of the frolics as they could."

A knock on the door surprised Arie from her daydream. Drying her hands on the towel, she went to answer the door. A trim, little old woman with ivory-white hair stood on the step. "Hello! Do come in," Arie invited her.

"Hi! I guess you don't know me, but I'm Capp's wife," the lady said with a friendly smile. "My name's Myrna, and I came to meet my neighbors."

Arie gasped. "Capp's wife? What a surprise!"

She pulled out a chair for Myrna and sat down, too. "I don't believe I knew that he had a wife who was still living."

"I am living! I left him ten years ago, when he became so terribly bitter. I guess he got a lot worse after I left him, but I just couldn't stand it anymore.

"He tracked me down after the old house collapsed in the wind. He asked me to come back. I told him I would if he'd build a new house and forget his bitter grudge. He promised that. Now, thanks to you Amish people, the house is finished, and here I am."

She took out her handkerchief and wiped a few tears from her eyes. "We're going back to our church now, too." Myrna smiled through her tears. "Capp seems like a changed man."

"I'm so glad." Arie was moved and genuinely happy. "I guess our prayers for Capp have been answered. Sometimes God moves in a mysterious way, his wonders to perform."

"That's true," Myrna nodded. "It will mean so much to us to have good neighbors. All these years I've had such a longing to come back to see the chestnut ridge. You see, I grew up right here in this house you're living in, and I spent many hours roaming the ridge when I was a child. Then when I married Capp, I moved to that place and lived there ever since, until ten years ago."

"Well!" Arie was astonished. "So you've played in the shade of the chestnut trees, and probably your children did, too."

"No, we never had any children," Myrna informed her. "After both of my parents died, the farm was sold. Before I was married, around 1930, that terrible chestnut blight struck the ridge, and every one of the chestnut trees died. My dad later planted more chestnut trees, and they flourished for awhile, but eventually they succumbed to the blight, too, and all died.

"Then later he planted the horse chestnut trees that are on the ridge now. Of course, there have always been lots of other trees there too, but there are no real chestnut trees."

"Oh! And all this time we thought they were chestnut trees! Wait till I tell Joe!" Arie was astounded.

"Well, I'd best be getting back to my house." Myrna got up to leave.

"It sure is a nice little house," Arie said. "You know, we always thought Capp was . . . uh . . . rather poor, living in such a shabby house and all. But now he built such a neat little house. I guess we were wrong."

"Poor!" Myrna scoffed. "Pooh, he was a miser, that's what. He always had a sizable bank account ever since I've know him. When I left, I guess he just hoarded his money instead of making repairs. But as I said, he's a changed man. I thank you from the bottom of my heart for all you did for him. Come over and visit us sometime."

"We will," Arie promised. She watched as Myrna got into her car and drove out the lane, over the bridge, and into Capp's lane.

"Will wonders ever cease!" she marveled. "Wait till I tell Joe! It will be so nice to have a woman like Myrna for a close neighbor!"

That afternoon, Joe harnessed Chief and led him out to hitch to the trottin' buggy. They were going to town for groceries, and he needed some things at the hardware store, too. Lady, their new collie pup, frisked around the horse's legs. Joe shooed the pup away, for fear he would be stepped on.

Arie came hurrying out the walk, still tying her bonnet strings and pinning her shawl. "We'd better *mach's schnell* (make it snappy), or we could get wet."

Joe glanced at the sky. "It does look for rain sometime today. Maybe it will hold off till we get home. I have the wheel off the carriage to repair it, so we have to use this rig."

As Arie climbed into the buggy, a mother cat jumped out from under the seat where she had been hiding. "Well, where did she come from?" Arie exclaimed in surprise. "It's a good thing she jumped off when she did or she'd have gone along to town." After they were out on the road and over the narrow bridge, they heard a soft meow from under the seat.

"Was in die Welt (what in the world)?" Joe muttered. He peered under the seat and began to laugh. "Look down there," he told Arie.

215

Arie bent to look, then burst out laughing. "A nest of kittens!" Five small wiggly creatures crawled over each other on a feed bag. "We'd better not stay long, or mama cat will be worried and the babies will be crying for milk."

A mile down the road, the sky began to darken and drops of rain began to fall.

"Oh, no, I'm afraid we're in for it now," Joe declared. "Shall we turn around and go home?"

Rain began to splash down in earnest, and soon it was a regular downpour.

"I guess we'd better turn around," Arie said. "I'm afraid my bonnet will be ruined."

Just then a truck passed and stopped in front of them. The driver got out and hurried back to them with a large piece of plastic. "Here's something to help keep you dry," he said, in a friendly, booming voice. "You'd be soaked in no time at all."

"Oh, thanks a lot," Joe responded, and Arie added her thanks, too. The man helped to spread the plastic over them. "There you are, snug as a bug in a rug." Then laughing, he went back to his truck, and with a wave of his hand, he drove off.

"My, was he ever nice," Arie declared. "He wouldn't have had to run out in the rain for us like that."

"A right friendly chap," Joe agreed. "We sure can't complain about the people in this area. They're really friendly and respectful. And now that Capp has reformed, it's better than ever."

"We sure have a lot to be thankful for," Arie agreed. "Capp has made another change for the better since

Myrna is here with him. You said he even decided that he's satisfied with the boundary line the way it is. It's almost unbelievable."

"Our first growing season at Chestnut Ridge Acres is about over," Joe remarked. "We've been blessed with plenty of rainfall and good growing weather. We've had a bumper crop, and the cows are doing well.

"In spite of all our ups and downs, we survived. We can be thankful that Amish aid paid us for most of the loss of the four cows and the bull."

"Yes, it seems like we've had quite a few bumps and hard knocks, but God took care of us through it all," Arie said gratefully and humbly. "Your beard grew back in nicely, too," she teased him. "I like you better this way. You're quite a man!"

They were huddled under the plastic, with the rain beating down on top, with Joe's arms outside to guide Chief with the reins, and with a nest of kittens under the seat. Arie felt happy and secure.

Yes, life at Chestnut Ridge Acres had been rocky at times, with its share of trials, *Heemweh* (homesickness), and anxieties. She knew it wouldn't all be roses in the future, either. But it was home, sweet home, and they hoped that someday the old homestead would ring with the laughter and happy sounds of a house full of children.

Arie felt as if their cup of happiness was full and running over. There would be heartaches, too, mingling with the sweetness and joys of the paths ahead of them. Hand in hand, they would travel life's pathways together.

The Author

THE author's pen name is Carrie Bender. She is a member of an old order group. With her husband and children, she lives among the Amish in Lancaster County, Pennsylvania. Her books are listed on page 2.

Bender is the popular author of the Whispering Brook Series, books about fun-loving Nancy Petersheim as she grows up surrounded by her close-knit Amish family, friends, and church community. This series is for children and a general audience.

The Miriam's Journal Series is also well appreciated by a wide reading public. These stories in journal form are about a middle-aged Amish woman who for the first time finds love leading to marriage. Miriam and Nate raise a lively family and face life with faith and faithfulness. Bender portrays their ups and downs through the seasons, year after year.

Miriam's Cookbook presents recipes for the tasty, hearty meals of Amish everyday life. They are spiced with fitting excerpts from Bender's books.

The Dora's Diary Series, also in journal form, tells about Miriam and Nate's adopted daughter going out with the young folks, becoming a schoolteacher, and growing close to a special boyfriend.

Herald Press (616 Walnut Ave., Scottdale, PA 15683) has received many fan letters for Carrie Bender. Readers say they have "thoroughly enjoyed" her "heartwarming" books. Her writing is "like a breath of fresh air," telling of "loyalty, caring, and love of family and neighbors." They give "a comforting sense of peace and purpose."

Library Journal says, "Bender's writing is sheer poetry. It leads readers to ponder the intimate relationship of people and nature."